KU-181-387

LOCKWOOD LIONS

The Lockwood High cheer squad has it *all*—sass, looks, and all the right moves. But everything isn't always as perfect as it seems. Because where there's cheer, there's drama. And then there are the ballers—hot, tough, and on point. But what's going to win out—life's pressures or their NFL dreams?

BALLER
Swag

ER Stone has all the scouts jocking him.
*It's when ER loses it all that he realizes
he wants it all.*

GOT PRIDE

Stephanie Perry Moore
& Derrick Moore

BALLER SWAG

All That

No Hating

Do You

Be Real

Got Pride

SADDLEBACK
EDUCATIONAL PUBLISHING
www.sdlback.com

Copyright © 2012 by Saddleback Educational Publishing

All rights reserved. No part of this book may be reproduced in any form or by any means, electronic or mechanical, including photocopying, recording, scanning, or by any information storage and retrieval system, without the written permission of the publisher. SADDLEBACK EDUCATIONAL PUBLISHING and any associated logos are trademarks and/or registered trademarks of Saddleback Educational Publishing.

ISBN-13: 978-1-61651-888-2
ISBN-10: 1-61651-888-X
eBook: 978-1-61247-622-3

Printed in Guangzhou, China
0812/CA21201149

16 15 14 13 12   1 2 3 4 5

To Tina Crittenden and Angela King

We would have never gotten to experience football from the unique perspective we now see it had it not been for you two. Thank you for giving us one of the best gifts of our lives, as you believed in us from the start. You both are strong ladies making the world a better place with how you give and help others daily. We hope you are proud of this story.

You are women we are proud to call family …
thanks and love!

ACKNOWLEDGEMENTS

Sometimes things happen in life that you aren't proud of. When things don't turn out like you plan, you may sulk, cry, or sometimes want to die. It's even tougher when you're a male on a team, and you feel like you let everyone down. You're supposed to hold it together and not be vulnerable. However, who said feeling something was wrong?

Of course, we all want happy endings: to be the one who leads our team to victory or to be proud of your folks. However, pride comes from within. It's not what happens that makes you proud, but it is celebrating all that you've come through to accomplish big goals. Pride is also deciding to stay up when life knocks you down. You don't go along to get along. No, you stand—even if alone—to make everyone around you better. Like milk helps the body grow, pride helps your character mature. Got pride?

Here is an immense thanks to those who help us remain proud of our work.

Acknowledgements

To our parents: Dr. Franklin and Shirley Perry Sr. and Ann Redding, because you lived your life in such a way that made us proud … we got pride.

To our publisher, especially the Saddleback office staff, because you made sure we were well taken care of every step of the writing way … we got pride.

To our extended family: brothers, Dennis Perry and Victor Moore, sister, Sherry Moore, godparents, Walter and Marjorie Kimbrough, Jim and Deen Sanders, young nephews, Franklin Perry III, Kadarius Moore, and godsons, Danton Lynn, Dakari Jones, and Dorian Lee, because you are our family … we got pride.

To our assistants: Shaneen Clay and Keisha King, because you worked overtime to make sure this got done … we got pride.

To our friends who mean so much: Paul and Susan Johnson, Chan and Laurie Gailey, Antonio and Gloria London, Chett and Lakeba Williams, Jay and Deborah Spencer, Bobby and Sarah Lundy, Harry and Torian Colon, Byron and Kim Forest, Chris and Jenell Clark, Donald and Deborah Bradley, because you inspire us … we got pride.

To our teens: Dustyn, Sydni, and Sheldyn, because you're soaring on your own … we got pride.

To the media specialists, school administrators, teachers, and educational companies across the country who support us, especially the folks at Mataoca High School in Virginia, Monroe High School in Georgia, and Jeff Davis High School in Alabama, because you educated us and cared so ... we got pride

To our new readers, who we know will excel at reading, because you are on book five of the Baller Swag series ... we got pride.

And to our Heavenly Father, who we're most proud to know, because we are yours ... we got pride.

CHAPTER 1

Heated Exchange

Boom! Clash! Bang! I turned quickly as I heard someone hitting and kicking one of the gym locker doors. Turns out it was mine. Then it was slammed shut.

Finally, I was eligible after transferring from Grovehill High School in East Cobb after the first game of the year to Lockwood High School. Tonight was going to be my time to shine, kick the ball through the uprights, get the field goal *and* the extra points. Whatever my team needed, I was ready to suit up and play. All I wanted to do was concentrate, listen to a little music, and loosen up, but the former kicker, Brick Bailey, got in my face and wouldn't let me.

"Why are you doing that to my locker?" I snapped. "I'm real tired of people trying me."

I was the white dude at a black school. There were only a few white guys on the team. Most days someone at the school did not let me forget the color of my skin.

"Coach just told me I'm not playing. Said he's giving my spot to the cracker. I may have missed kicks, but I was getting it. Dang," Brick snarled, as if I was the one making the decisions.

I just threw my hands up in the air and stepped back. I didn't want no beef. Brick needed to take up his frustration with Coach. However, he didn't leave me alone. He stepped toward me.

Brick huffed, "Being the kicker is *my* job. We've won every game this season. I'm not gonna let you come in here and take it."

While I appreciated Brick knowing what he wanted in life, he really needed to look in the mirror and be objective. Coach Strong would not make me the starting kicker, after missing most of the season, if there wasn't a significant need for change. Our school was undefeated; that was true, but it certainly wasn't because Brick did anything to make it that way. He missed field goals and extra points. We had the craziest scores this season because of his bad execution. The last team we played made fun of our kicking game on the Internet by posting a message that said, "We may have problems, but a kicker is not one of them."

Besides, if Coach allowed Brick to play, did the jerk think he would be better than what he had been? I was cutting him slack because I knew it had to be hard getting pulled from the starting line and watching your job get taken by someone else. However, this wasn't the first time this happened on the team this year. Coach had already switched out our underperforming defensive back for Amir Knight, a guy who quite possibly could play in the NFL *right now*. He was that good.

Coach was trying to win the state title. He was doing whatever was necessary to make that happen. This was a big boy's game, not pee-wee football, and since the program was so highly thought of by college coaches, my dad got me in this school.

Having someone go off on me was not my cup of tea, and frankly, I wasn't a tea drinker at all. I mean, I was starting to fit in. I had a few dudes on the team I was bonding with, and now that I was getting comfortable, I refused to let anyone make me shiver.

Brick just had to try me. He put his hand on my chest. That was it. I took his hand and bent it backward. I was ready to pop it out of its socket and crush his fingers. I wasn't an angry kid, but at seventeen, I had gone through some things. Brick and every other teammate of mine needed to know the white boy had backbone.

"Ouch, ER. Dang! Stone, man, that hurt," Brick yelped. "Let up my hand. Let go or you're gonna break it."

"Think about that before you get in my face next time," I threatened.

Landon and Leo, two guys on defense who I had started hanging out with, stepped in. It was cool they wanted to stop the altercation. They broke us apart.

"C'mon, man," Landon got in my face and said. "He ain't worth it. You got to go out there and do this. You know Coach Strong's crazy, and he will kick both of you off the team. Then what we gonna do?"

"Yeah, what we gonna do? I sure can't get out there and kick," Leo said, trying to make me laugh, but none of this was funny.

Landon turned to Leo and said, "Talk to Brick, man. Tell him what's up."

"Yeah, dude, you can't be mad at ER. You gotta be mad at Coach. He's the one who made the change. And Brick, be real, dude, you know you ain't kicking like you need to be out there. But if you really think you deserve to start, then make the argument with the coach. But I don't know."

Brick kept blowing off steam and said, "Why you taking up for the white boy, Leo? He don't understand our world. He should have stayed on the other side of Atlanta."

Tired of the bull and pampering, I yelled, "Why does this have to be about race? You weren't handling yours. If I am the better kicker, then that's just the way it is. I could be purple and gold, like the school colors. I get the job done and the job is mine."

"Well, you're talking a good game. You been making some kicks in practice, but wait till you get out there. I been watching you, thinking you're the one who's gonna have the job. You over analyze. What will be the strength of your kicks when you get out there tonight? With the crowd going wild, I bet you won't be able to relax in your lil' honky tonk beats and drown out the world. Your kicks won't be no better than mine," Brick predicted. I let his criticism seep into my brain.

"C'mon, man. C'mon," Landon said. It was time for us to head out on the field and warm up for the game.

We won the toss and decided to defer. On the opening kickoff, I ran, geared up to kick the ball to the opposing team. As I ran to the ball, all the stuff Brick had said to me came rushing back. I remembered him saying, "When you're out there and the crowd's going wild, you're going to freeze up."

I felt my leg swing back to swing forward, and I could feel that I actually touched the pigskin. The problem wasn't the power, it was that the execution was off. The ball rolled out of bounds on our thirty-five-yard line, and because it went out of bounds, we got a penalty. The team got the ball on our forty-five. Coach was livid when I got over to the benches.

"Told y'all. What did I say? He ain't no better than me," Brick screamed.

My teammates were ticked too. Brick wasn't the only one talking about me, but for some reason, his voice rang loud and clear. He'd messed up all season. I was due one error.

Coach grabbed my helmet and said, "Stone, where is your head? What the heck kind of kick was that?"

At that moment, I felt like a failure. This was homecoming. The stadium was so full there were no places for fans to sit. Tons of alumni were there, and so was the press because we were doing so well. The game was even being televised on Georgia Public Broadcast, and on the opening play, I failed to deliver for my team.

Things intensified on the very next play. The opposing team's quarterback threw the ball to their wide receiver, but Amir stepped in the way and ran for the touchdown. Just like that, I was called to go back out on the field and get the extra point.

"You're gonna miss it," Brick whispered to me. Then he pushed past me, hitting my shoulder hard.

I had to jog about forty yards to where I needed to stand to make the point. However, I felt like I was running for miles. In the back of my head, I didn't want to reach my position. I didn't want to get in place for that kick.

The center hiked the ball to the holder, who placed it on the tee—turned just right so the strings wouldn't be facing me. I gave it a solid shot, but the ball didn't go through the uprights. I dropped to my knees, angry at myself. Landon picked me up and helped me jog off to the sidelines. Hearing roars of boos, Coach Strong came up and got in my face.

Coach hollered, "Look, you are *the Man*."

"No, Coach, take me out."

"You are our kicker, Stone. I don't know what's going on with you. You came out a little timid, but I know what you can do. Dang it, lose the goose bumps and shake off the cobwebs. It's time to play ball!"

"Put in Bailey, Coach. Put in Bailey."

"No, you're my kicker. Stop the nonsense and let's play. You can do this, son," he said. He looked me square in the eyes.

He didn't know it, but that conversation helped me. The next three kicks I was sent out for, I made. His belief in me turned me around.

We won the game. Again, the Lions came out victorious. This time the kicker contributed. I was overjoyed.

On the ride home, my dad took out some of the joy. "I'm just trying to figure out what happened to you in the beginning of the game."

Of all the things for my father to focus on, he was talking about my bad kicking, not the extra points I made or the good field position my kicks ended up putting us in. No, he was on me and I resented him. I just looked out the window, wishing I would have driven my own car.

"No need to sit over there and get all wimpy. It's time to play now, son. We don't have time for nerves or mistakes. It practically took all semester to get your tail out there to perform. I was sitting next to three scouts, one guy from Georgia, one guy from Georgia Tech, and one from Auburn. I think a Clemson man might have been there too. There are so many great athletes on this team; you have to make plays, not mistakes."

"Okay, Dad, got you," I said, hoping he would understand that I needed him to hush.

I knew what was at stake. He told me time and time again that he didn't have money to send me to college. My grades were good but not good enough with the higher restrictions on the Hope Scholarship.

"When you missed that extra point, they all were writing down notes and shaking their heads," he nagged.

"Dad, they could have been writing down anything."

"You're missing the point, son. They weren't writing down this is the boy we need to bring into our program, trust me. Don't be an idiot. The best thing you got going is that you stick out like a sore thumb being one of the only white boys on this team. You did make three extra points to redeem yourself."

"Did you see them writing down something then?" I asked sarcastically.

"Oh see, you're trying to antagonize me. It's not gonna be funny when you're sitting here with me in a couple of years because you couldn't get into anybody's school."

"Dad, this season is really a wash because I wasn't able to play. Basketball season is right around the corner. I can get a scholarship in that."

"It's gonna be harder for you to do that, son," he said. My dad had a habit of breaking down life in black and white, which truly frustrated me. "Don't look disappointed. You know most D1 basketball scholarships do not go to boys who look like you. Quarterbacks, offensive lineman, kickers, and baseball players all day and night—you can close your eyes and get one of those jobs."

I didn't want to argue with him. He wasn't a bully, but he definitely loved to flex his muscles. He always thought he was right.

He had baggage. He and my mom got a divorce a few years ago. He had been living out of the state. When he came back this summer, she didn't put up much of a fight for me to go live with him.

I resented him for leaving. I resented her for letting me go. Though I tried to get through my anger, every now and then it arose. When my dad told me I couldn't do something or showed me that he really wasn't that proud, I got heated. I really wanted to prove him wrong more than I wanted to do right for myself.

I remembered my mom talking to some of her friends about my dad's woes. He used to have a big-time corporate job. When the company got sued for not hiring minorities, one of the first white males they let go was my dad. Now he worked for Walmart, overseeing several stores in the Metro-Atlanta area.

Ever since he got on the wrong end of a discrimination claim, it was like he was always calculating where color played a factor in job security. I could also sense that there was something else going on with him. He never went out. He didn't have a social life. A few years back, I wished he and my mom would get back together, but I now realized that definitely wasn't ever going to happen. I just wanted the man to be happy, find somebody, branch out, not be such a coach potato, and not scrutinize every area of my life, but it was what it was, I guess. He was right. I needed to get a scholarship so that in a year and a half, I would be out of his house. At the rate we were going, we were not going to make it together much longer.

When we pulled up to my house, my dad hit the steering wheel and growled through his teeth. "Dang it! Why is *she* here?"

I quickly looked at the driveway and saw my mom's car. I didn't mind seeing her, but like my father, I certainly didn't want to hear the two of them arguing all night. He didn't even want to pull in the driveway. I gave him a look like, *Dad, she's already seen you. You might as well pull in.*

He grunted. The garage went up and he pulled in. Before we could get out, she was out of her car.

"You go talk to Mom because I don't want to talk to her," he said emphatically. "Keep her out here. I don't want her in my house."

"Dad, really?" I said, alluding to the fact that he was going overboard.

"You don't have to like it, but you do have to respect my decision," he said with a flat and angry voice.

"Hello," my mom greeted.

"Hey, Mom," I replied.

Ever chipper, she said, "I just came by to see if you wanted to come and hang out with me this weekend."

"You want him to stay over?" my dad butted in despite what he had just said.

I wanted to say, "Nah, Dad, you didn't want to talk to Mom. You weren't interested in what she had to say." Of course I knew not to mess with him.

"He's not going over to your place. No, uh-uh," he declared.

"Stone!" Mom yelled. "Don't fight me on this. I want to spend some time with my son, and I've let you keep him from me for too long."

He grabbed my mom's arm and pulled her a few feet away from me. "Don't make me go there," he growled. "I will if you push me."

"Stop! Dad," I shouted.

He put his hand out and ordered, "Stay back over there, son. You know what? Go on inside. Your mom and I will talk about this."

"Dad, I'm not going anywhere. Why are you grabbing her arm like that?"

"Do I need to tell him why?" my father asked my mother.

"Okay, okay. Son, just let us talk," my mom agreed. I had no idea why my dad would have the upper hand.

I was clueless about what my parents were discussing. As they stepped further away from me, I couldn't hear what they were saying. However, I could see it was confrontational, as my dad's arms went all over the place and my mom's were folded.

Was it such a big deal if I went to stay with my mom? I was seventeen years old. Didn't I have some say in what happened in my own life? Being that we weren't going to watch film with Coach Strong until Sunday, and I knew Grovehill had a big game coming up against their cross-town rivals, McEachern, I decided I wanted to go.

My folks were getting on my nerves, so I said, "Hey, hey, I wanna go to Mom's. It's just overnight, Dad."

"Son, let us handle this," my dad said.

"No, Dad, I'm not gonna let y'all handle it. I'm here with you every day. I haven't seen Mom since August. It's November. I didn't think she wanted to be around me, but obviously, that's not the case. I'll come back tomorrow night after the game."

"Lydia, promise *that* won't be a distraction for my son?" he asked, eluding to something deep.

"You've got my word," she said, confusing me again.

"Fine, go," he said.

"I'll wait for you to get your things so you can follow me. Plus, I know Jillian would love to see you tomorrow." My mom smiled.

"Lydia, I don't understand you," my dad sighed.

I took a deep breath. I really needed to break up with Jillian. I found a way to reduce the time I saw her to once a month, but she was starting to annoy me by telling me how much I was letting her down in the boyfriend department. She was one of the cutest girls at Grovehill, a competition cheerleader, and a straight-A student, but she was a little wicked. We hooked up because of a bet last year. My boy Gage and I made a bet to see who could snag her. I won. Or maybe I lost because sometimes you need to be careful what you ask for.

Thirty minutes later, I was following my mom to her place. A part of me wanted to ask what was up between my parents. A bigger part of me didn't want to know. I didn't like that they were keeping something from me, but I guess I'd find out when I needed to. Bonding with my mom, preparing myself for the upcoming play-off game, and figuring out what I was going to do with Jillian was enough hot stuff to handle without adding more to my already full plate.

"So what are you planning to do about Jillian, son?" my mom asked me the next evening.

"Huh?" I asked. She'd caught me off guard; I was trying to get ready to head to Grovehill's football game.

Did she know I was contemplating breaking up with Jillian? Was a mother's intuition truly that strong? Or was she guessing?

"Are you going to pick her up? Do you have special plans after the game?" she questioned.

I wanted to ask, "Mom, why do you care?" But instead I said, "I really haven't thought about it. I'm just meeting her there."

"Honey, I know we haven't talked lately."

"Mom, we haven't talked at all. I can't believe you didn't call me in all these months."

"You have a cell phone too, ER. You can pick it up and call me."

"Yeah, but when you didn't put up a fight when I left, I didn't think you wanted to talk to me. You have custody of me, Mom. That's why there's this issue about me getting eligibility. You wouldn't relinquish custody to Dad. So even though he's my father, legally I wasn't supposed to be living with him, and you wouldn't help. You did not want to transfer rights, but you didn't fight for me to stay here. I'm real confused and now you wanna talk to me about Jillian? She's just some girl. Honestly, we have bigger issues that we have not dealt with."

My mom sank to her rocker. "Yes, ER, you have a point. I was just asking about Jillian because she called me a couple of times crying, saying how you didn't care anymore. But you know what? You're right. That's your business. I want to talk about this frustration that you have with thinking I didn't want you. That's so far from the truth."

"Okay, Mom. Am I fabricating the story here? You didn't fight dad when he took me from you. You made sure I was packed up and ready to go fast enough. Am I making this up?" I asked.

"There are a lot of other circumstances; stuff I don't want to get into. While I know you desperately wanted to play football, and the coach here was angry that you left, I didn't want to give up my rights that I fought so hard for during the divorce."

"So what made you finally come around?" I asked.

"The season was almost over, and the Lockwood Lions were doing very well except in the kicking position."

Stunned I asked, "How do you—?"

"How do I know?" she responded. "Because I went to a couple of the games. I'm surprised you didn't spot me because I stood out like a sore thumb. I saw you pacing the sidelines. It looked like your heart was broken into a million pieces, and I knew I was the one who could fix things."

"So why didn't you say anything? Why didn't you come up to me? Why didn't you—"

"What? Tell you good job tonight for the three field goals you made? Shoot, one was practically a forty-six-yarder."

"You were there last night?"

"I'm your mother, ER," she said. She placed her hand on my face. "I shouldn't have to tell you that I'm looking out for you."

"You know what, Mom? You talk about being there for me, coming to my games and stuff, like it's some big sacrifice. So you take a little time out of your day to watch your son. Big deal. *My* life is the one that keeps getting turned upside down. It hasn't been easy, and I don't see you really trying to help me."

"I know, I know. I don't know why your dad wants you to go there. He thinks it's best, though I question why."

Defending my new school, I said, "Because it's a great school. I'm definitely learning the world is more diverse than I ever knew it was. My teammates at Lockwood have a bond that goes way deeper than just football. I see them going through it and laying down everything for each other. Right now, I feel they care more about me than my parents do."

"That's not fair, ER," she said, looking away.

"What's not fair is me coming here and thinking that we could be honest, and that maybe for once you would see things from my point of view. But you have your own agenda. Hanging out with Jillian? Are you serious, Mom? I don't even know why I took the time to come out here."

"ER, there is something going on with me that you don't understand."

"Well then, talk to me, Mom. And it needs to be pretty heavy. I have one friend whose mom has cancer. She can be there for her son. I have another friend whose mom is homeless. She's there for her son. One lady just found out her son was molested years ago, but instead of abandoning him, she's there for him to work through it. So what's going on with you that makes it too much to handle to be there for your son? Huh? You're not saying anything … right … nothing."

I picked up my keys and headed to the football game, slamming the door behind me. She did not even try to follow me. I really didn't want to attend the game at that point, but I drove there anyway. As if there was tracking device on me, Jillian called. Looking at the phone, I sighed.

After hearing her nag me, I said, "I'll be at the game, Jillian. We will find each other."

"So you're not gonna pick me up? We're not gonna go together?" she whined.

Without caring, I said, "No."

She had manipulated me for far too long.

"What's wrong? What did I do?"

"Talking to my mother, Jillian, really? Like she controls me? Why would you make her think I'm treating you bad?"

"You hardly ever call. You never take me out."

"And that's treating you bad? Maybe we just need some—"

"No, no, no! Don't say it, okay? I'll just see you at the game. Gosh, it's just that everybody is looking forward to you coming. It's on Facebook. People miss you, and I thought you would be walking in on my arm."

What was I doing here? What did I even miss about it? At this school, a lot of people cared more about their image than what kind of a person they were. I even had a feeling my best friend, Gage, was happy I didn't have many stats this year. *He* wanted to be the guy who made the biggest impression on college scouts.

There were a few other teammates I'd been tight with here. But ever since I lost my eligibility, most of them hadn't called to see if I was okay or even to say they felt bad for me.

I decided it was good for me to be at this game and to see that maybe I'd outgrown Grovehill. Lockwood was best for me now. My new buddies at Lockwood were genuine.

As soon as I realized that I was content with my school, I saw my new coach. Coach Strong and our defensive coordinator, Coach Grey, were walking toward me. I had forgotten we were set to play Grovehill the very next week.

"Great game yesterday, son," Coach Strong said to me. "Really appreciate you hanging in there with me, keeping your head on straight, and doing what we knew you could. I thank you for the opportunity to coach you, son.

"So you're not here scouting the competition; you already know how this team operates. You here for a girlfriend, maybe?" Coach Strong teased. "Next week's gonna be tough. We're undefeated and I want to keep it that way. So don't hang out too long."

"No, sir."

"All right, son. See you for film tomorrow."

"Yes, sir," I responded.

I went to the concession stand, and I saw a beautiful sight. It wasn't Jillian, it was a girl from my new school. She had the prettiest skin I had ever seen. She was glowing. Her hair was long and curly. She was a cheerleader at Lockwood. Raven? Rina? No, Randal. Yeah, Randal was her name.

I suddenly realized that my heart was going pitter patter for someone I really didn't know. It kind of scared me. Then I felt an urge to go over and calm her when I saw a shocked look come over her face. Two girls had started kissing right in front of her.

Right then, I knew I needed to find Jillian. We needed to talk. Our stuff needed to be over. It wasn't a fun conversation to have, but it was about time to have that heated exchange.

CHAPTER 2

Diminish Pressure

It was excruciating sitting there watching Grovehill's game with Jillian. I wanted to pay attention to my boys, their moves, the plays, the scores, the hits, and the kicks, but all she kept doing was gossiping, like I was one of her girl-friends. She enjoyed dishing on other people.

"So you know Becca and Savannah have come out of the closet. They practically do it in school every day. So sad for Savannah 'cause lots of guys wanted to take her out. Now if they try and flirt with her, Becca would probably kill them. Oh my gosh, look at that poor girl's style.

She shouldn't have even come out the house in that tacky outfit."

"Everybody might not have money to buy something new, Jillian," I vented. I was way past annoyed.

"Then they should stay home. I can't believe your school is coming here next week. How can you even stand to go to school with hoodlums? I can see how Randal fits in, but you? You should never mix with mutts."

Trying not to be rude, I said, "Okay, Jillian. I got you. Can I just watch the game?"

"What? I'm just being truthful. Please don't tell me you've gotten sensitive over there with the charity cases."

"Can you stop all that?" I commanded, seriously frustrated with her.

I was really annoyed that she was so judgmental and for no reason. What had anybody at Lockwood ever done to her? So what that Lockwood was coming to Grovehill for a football game? That's why there was a home and visitor side; the two did not have to mingle.

"Okay, okay, don't be so touchy," she said, sliding her arm underneath my elbow.

I tried to wrestle away during the fourth quarter, but she clenched on tighter. That girl would not let me go. I wanted to shout hallelujah when the game was over.

Huffing, I rose and simply said, "Game over. All right, Jillian, I'll see you later."

"Wait, where you going? You gotta take me home."

"I'm staying with my mom. I told her I wouldn't be out too late."

"I'm sure your mother is not going to care if you're hanging out with me," Jillian said. She was a piece of work, truly confident and right on.

For some reason my mother thought she was precious. In my mom's eyes, Jillian was the perfect girl. If she only knew how sneaky and pushy Jillian was, she wouldn't try so hard to get us together.

"I talked to your mom," Jillian drawled. "She's excited we're gonna hang out some. You're not going to be out all night, but Gage and the guys want to party it up tonight. Don't be a pooper. The first thing I need to do is get you a beer so you can unwind some."

"I don't drink," I voiced in an insulted tone.

"Can't you see that's probably the problem?" she suggested. She kissed me on the cheek, took my hand, and paraded me through the crowd.

I wasn't a groupie. I wasn't a girl. So I did not like that Jillian took me down by the locker room for me to hang out and wait for the football players.

"You said we were going to the party. Can't we just see everyone there?" I asked.

"Ugh, ER, you're really annoying me. Do I need to call you Edgar, 'cause I know how much you hate that name. Maybe that'll make you straighten up, Edgar Remington Stone."

Why did this girl like pushing all my buttons? Why I put up with it was actually the more pertinent question. It was probably because she was the first girl to kiss me in places girl's lips weren't supposed to go.

Finally, when I got her to agree to leave, I felt someone hit me in the back super hard. "Ouch!"

"That new school of yours didn't turn you into a sissy, did it? If so, we're gonna have a good time next week whuppin' y'all's tails," my old buddy Gage Wolf said to me.

"Nah, be happy about the victory you got tonight, 'cause that's the last one you're gonna see this season," I told the arrogant guy.

"We may not be undefeated, but you guys might not be either after you play next week, so hold up on being a fortune teller. You might need to wait to read all about it and get your facts right. We've been waiting on Lockwood all year."

"Don't pay ole Gage no mind," my other partner and wide receiver Kelly Cunningham grabbed me around the neck and said.

"Kelly! What's up, boy?"

Jillian and I were catching up with some of my old teammates. I could see out of the corner of my eye something interesting going on that gave me pause. Gage had his hand on Jillian's back pocket. I couldn't say he was squeezing, but he didn't have any business doing that in the first place. When I looked up from her backside to her face, I caught her eye looking my way. Once she saw me looking, she batted her lashes at Gage.

"I'll talk to y'all later," I announced to Kelly.

Kelly responded, "You not gonna come hang out with us, ER? Beer's on us, man."

"Nah, I got film tomorrow. I need to take it in, but I'll see you guys next week." Then I quickly walked over to Jillian and said, "Let's go."

"You gotta be so abrupt? What's wrong with you?" Gage, the Giants' quarterback, looked at me and said sternly.

I could tell the tightness we once shared had evaporated like fog on a car window when the defroster is turned on. He wanted to control my actions with his crude behavior. However, I had my own mind, and now that I wasn't in his company daily, I could see the leader of the team was leading people astray.

"I want to go to the party, ER. I don't want to go home. Since I'm not the only person right here going, Gage can take me."

"No, we need to hang out," I said. "Let's go, Jillian."

"Okay. Bye, Gage," she said quickly, not giving me any more tension. "Why you walking all fast? Hold up."

I wasn't going to slow down. I wasn't calm. I needed to talk to her. I didn't like being played.

"Why are you acting so mean? And if we aren't going straight home, where are we going?"

We got in the car and drove. I kept quiet. There was a park by the elementary school down the street. I pulled in to the parking lot.

"Let's talk," I told her after I parked.

"You want to honestly do that? Great."

Getting right to it, I said, "What's going on with you and Gage? I mean, I can tell by the way he was looking at you and the way you just let his hand roam anywhere that there's something going on. What's that about?"

"Ooh, somebody's jealous," she said. She came over to my side of the car, reached over me, leaned my seat back, and took off her sweater.

While the sexy lace bra she had on was extremely attractive, I was focused. I wanted an answer. So I gently took both my hands and pushed her body back to the passenger side.

"Come on, sweetie," she purred. She leaned back over and started kissing my neck.

"I wanna talk. I'm not trying to feel good. I just need you to be straight with me. I wanna understand. I haven't talked to you. I haven't seen you in—"

"Like that's my fault. Like I'm just sup-posed to sit and wait. What? What do you want me to say? That Gage doesn't like me? You said you saw his reaction. You're the one who came storming over there."

"For a reason."

"He's been after me, okay? Your best buddy wants me bad."

"Have you done anything to make him want that?" I questioned.

She reached over and slapped me. At that point, I was hot. She was a flirt, and she needed to be called on it.

"I'm sorry. I'm sorry. Forgive me," she said, kissing me all over my face.

It wasn't even that she hit me that hard, but it ticked me off. I had Jillian figured out. She wanted me to be angry. She wanted to push my buttons. She wanted to have sex with me, but I wasn't a hundred percent sure I'd be the only one. Once she saw that I wasn't going to give her what she wanted, she put back on her sweater and pouted. Not caring, I took her home.

"Coach always get on everybody that hard? I've never seen him that angry and rude," I said to Landon and Leo while we lifted weights after the intense meeting.

"Yeah, you just didn't have to hear it until now," Landon said, "since you weren't required to come to these Sunday meetings. I go to church and get all lifted up, then I'll have to come in and get all put down."

"For real, Coach Strong is my man and all, but he needs to chill," Leo uttered. "He talking about how I didn't rush the passer enough. Shoot, it's because I'm being double teamed. Even with that, I still did a couple moves that got me two sacks for the game, and he act like that ain't good enough."

Landon said, "Yeah, if he don't lay off of us, he's gonna lose everybody before the game Friday. We need to be unified going into the playoffs."

I just sat on the bench at that moment. There was too much pressure, and I felt like I needed a break from it all.

"You need me to spot you?" Landon asked.

"No, I'm just thinking," I said.

Leo popped me with a towel. "We're working out. You can't think in here. Let's go. Lean back. Let's do some reps."

"Talk about diminishing pressure," I said sarcastically to Leo.

"I'm just saying, Coach Strong got his agenda, but all of us have got ours too. Gotta think about scholarships, man. Even as a kicker you gotta have the right size. You're tall enough, but your butt is skinny as a bone."

"We're all gonna be skinny in a minute if we make this basketball team. You're still trying out, right, ER?" Landon asked.

"You can't ball, man," Leo teased.

"I ball better than I kick."

Leo clowned, "That ain't saying too much the way you missed that kick on Friday, dude."

"Oh see, you got jokes."

I looked over at Leo and he was texting. "Okay, so you're supposed to be spotting me, but you're on the phone."

Leo replied, "Nah, man, my girl just sent me a few pictures from the homecoming dance."

"He's all in love," Landon said, messing with him.

Leo quickly uttered, "Like I'm alone. You don't want to admit it, but you know you want my girl's sister."

"It's crazy y'all are dating twins," I said.

"I'm not dating," Landon argued, trying to be all tough.

"I got the better sister, ER," Leo said.

"Yeah, somebody he can boss around. I got the one with spunk. Who wants a pushover?" Landon defended.

"Who wants someone who's gonna talk back to you all the time?" Leo pressed.

Ending the back and forth, I cut in and said, "What's the difference? You both seem like you're happy."

"Right, right, right," they both said in unison. Their answer was so in sync that it was clear they were best buddies.

"I guess I need to be real with you guys," Landon said. "I hadn't really thought about what I feel for Eva. Leo's right. She's a handful, but like me, she's been broken. I don't know. Lately, it's been good to not have to go through stuff alone. At the homecoming dance, a part of me wanted to get her to some hotel and take her out of that sexy dress she was wearing."

"Dude, her dress wasn't sexy. It flared out like a poodle skirt," Leo snorted.

Like popping a soda can, Landon opened up. "I know, I know. That's just it. See, she's changing. It used to be that Eva would have worn the slim, tight thing, but she had it going on in something that was unflattering. It's weird. She turned me on it all kinds of ways. I guess what I'm saying is she's really becoming a part of me. I could feel that she was fragile, and I just wanted to hold her. I can't explain it, but as much as I try to deny it, I'm feeling something strong for the girl. I just can't go there, though."

"I ain't trying to throw around the word love," Leo said, "but I know that's what it is. When it's the right one, things just connect. This girl was bringing me food every night when she found out I was staying at the school. She got *shot* because of me. If she would have died, I don't know ... I just probably would have lived my whole life going after somebody for revenge."

"You got a girl, though. Right, ER?" Landon asked, remembering when I first came to the school I told him about Jillian.

Although I had someone, the feelings they were talking about: something extra, something real, something deep, something pure, something moving, and something strong wasn't what I had at all with Jillian. I had known for a while what we had was over, but for some reason, she didn't want to let go of it.

Being a gentleman, I obliged her request, though we weren't connecting. She had let me know that she was ready for sex, *and* that someone else was interested in her. By showing her I wasn't going to be manipulated by either one, I hoped she'd take her hooks out of me. Just because I wasn't going to Grovehill didn't mean I was okay with my girl getting with someone else—especially my old buddy. I wasn't ready to lose it to Jillian, just to get my kicks. I already felt trapped, and we hadn't even gone there. I could only imagine if we did, I'd probably never be able to get rid of her. That's certainly not what I wanted.

"You don't look like you like her too much," Leo commented, reading me right.

"Long story, guys. Forget me. Let's just say I hear guys all the time talking about how many notches they got on their belt. How many girls they've been with. How they got swag 'cause they're swinging. How they're not stable with anybody. I just think that's a cop out. I think, Landon, you're mind is telling you what society says, that boys will be boys. But your heart is telling you it's been through enough. It's ready for something good, and you should listen to it. If your stomach is growling, you eat, right?"

"What are you supposed to be, a philosopher or something?" Landon asked.

"One of y'all just spot me on these reps. Let me show you chumps that a kicker is just as strong as a defensive end and a wide receiver. Okay, well, maybe not a defensive end," I said, looking over at Leo squatting four hundred and fifty pounds without a spot.

"You better wait on us next time," Landon said to his boy.

Leo's cell phone rang. He put down the weights in a hurry. The boy was whipped. He went over and started talking to Ella.

So I turned to Landon and asked, "Did you really have a good time at the dance?"

"I did, man. I like her. The question is, what you gonna do?" he asked.

"Hey, you ain't even decided what *you* gonna do."

"I decided. You don't have to state your plan to make it happen." Landon added, "You know what I'm saying?"

"No, I don't."

"Well, you're basically telling me you got a girlfriend you don't like, but yet you won't break it off with her. Why? For appearances? Is that what your parents want? Is she the right kind of girl? Plenty of chicks over here been checking you out. They come to me thinking I got the scoop on what's up with your tail 'cause we're boys."

"I probably just need to get girls out of my mind totally. If I get rid of Jillian, I'm not looking for anyone else."

"I heard that."

"Just don't let her make you nervous on Friday night when we play there. We gotta win to keep our momentum going for the playoffs."

"That's what's up. No pressure, Landon."

"Nah, man, you can handle it," Landon said.

Leo hung up the phone and chimed in, "Yeah, you can handle it."

"Oh, see? Pressure from both of y'all."

Leo said, "Man, please, we are all a little nervous. Do you."

I really liked my new friends. We went deep without being vulnerable. We were there for each other. We kept it honest. It was a big deal.

"Man, why won't you come hang out with us?" Landon asked after we showered to clean up after our workout.

"Where you going?"

"To ... to go meet up with Brenton, Amir, and Blake," Landon said, tripping over his words.

Raising my eyebrows, I asked suspiciously, "Where, Landon?"

"Yeah, tell him where we going," Leo laughed.

"Regional cheerleading something or other," Landon replied.

I laughed. "Y'all really are in love. Tough football players going to a cheerleading meet?"

Jillian was in a regional cheer competition today as well, but I was certain it probably wasn't the same one. I never went to any of her meets, so I wouldn't feel bad if I didn't show up at this one. Lockwood was my new school, and if a lot of the football players were going to go to support the girls, then I was down. Besides, there was still tension at my house. I didn't want my dad asking a bunch of questions about my weekend with my mom. The longer I could put that off, the better.

So I said, "Yeah, I'll go. Can we eat something first?"

"Oh, we gonna eat," Leo said. "Plus, we need you to run interference with Blake and Brenton."

"What's going on with the two of them?" I asked.

"Blake wants his old girlfriend back," Landon told me.

I wasn't familiar with the story, but they were happy to fill me in. Like two heckling hens, Leo and Landon rambled off and told me how Charli, the cheerleading captain, used to date Blake. He broke up with her to date a girl on the dance team, but he regretted it when his cousin Brenton, who was a linebacker on our team, won Charli's heart. Except now it seemed Charli's heart might be wishy-washy. While Blake was cool, Brenton was too nice and didn't deserve to be jilted.

The event was actually interesting. Our girls did good. Randal impressed me when she was thrown high in the air. The event was going all day, but we weren't staying. As we were leaving the World Congress Center, Brenton was dragging. I could tell he was frustrated, and since Leo and Landon had enlightened me to the situation, I went up to him and asked if he needed to talk. He turned quickly, looking at me like he wanted to use me as a punching bag.

"Whoa, whoa. Sorry, man, I wasn't trying to startle you. I was just walking to the parking lot; thought we could talk."

Brenton threw up his hands and said, "I know I'm just ... I'm just stressed."

"Okay, can I be real with you? I think I know a little bit about what's going on. It's the Charli situation, right?"

"Oh, so everybody knows now?" Brenton uttered with a lot of angst.

"No."

"Yeah, white boy knows; everybody knows."

"Hey, man, why I gotta be the white boy? Why can't I just be your friend who cares? Is that such a big deal? You know what? Forget it."

"Nah, I'm sorry, man. See? She's got me all off kilter. I'm sorry. Forgive me."

Thinking about my girlfriend, I calmed down, "I understand, girls can definitely mess you up."

"I just liked her since middle school, and Blake treats her any kind of way. The fact that she's even entertaining being with him again is insulting. He's my cousin, and I know he's going through a lot because of his mom—"

"Yeah, cancer is hard," I said, feeling bad that I talked about how mean Coach Strong had been. "So basically, you're saying since your cousin has this big issue going on at home that he should get the girl no matter how he treats her?"

"Sort of, but I'm really saying if that's who the girl wants ..."

"But is that who she wants?"

"At the dance, ER, if you could have seen them two together, you wouldn't even need to ask me that question because you'd know the answer is yes. And there's something about being a fly on the wall, looking at two people gazing into each other's eyes when they don't even know you're looking. You see a chemistry going on between them that you know you and that other person don't have. It gets to you. What am I talking about? I'm just rambling, sounding like a fool."

"No, man, I got you." I reflected back on seeing Gage and Jillian.

Suddenly, I heard her voice. "Wait a minute, ER. I thought you weren't coming to this cheer competition because you told me you had other stuff to do."

I turned around and was busted. There stood Jillian with some of her cheerleading friends, all looking at me like, *Shame on you!* Brenton walked off, leaving me to get out of the shark-infested water on my own. When I thought about it, I actually didn't remember telling Jillian I couldn't go to a cheer competition, and I was a little ticked that she wanted to call me out in front of her friends.

"Look, if you wanna talk to me, I'm fine with it, but it needs to be alone."

She rolled her eyes at me. She turned around and talked to her friends. Then they stomped away with disgusted looks on their faces, like I hurt her or something.

"I didn't say I couldn't come to your meet."

"You didn't say you could, either."

"So why you acting like I dissed you or something?" I asked.

"Because you lied and told me you had to go to some meeting with your football coach. I'll bet you're here to support those tacky girls from your school. I mean, seriously, ER, what do you want, for us to be through or something?"

"You said it, I didn't."

"Oh, so that's what you want?" she cried, getting all dramatic.

And then all around me are girls, moms, and coaches looking at me like I was some bad boyfriend. It was becoming abundantly clear that what we had could not work. I had planned to tell her I wouldn't mind going to one of her competitions. I actually had a good time. Those Lockwood cheerleaders were a lot funkier than the other squads. They held their own. And though I was heading out, had I known that Grovehill was performing, I would have stayed to watch.

Now that she was putting me on blast, and I saw my boys coming around the corner for us to jet, I didn't have time for all this. And when I saw Gage walking behind them, checking Jillian out, I realized she was taken care of anyway. I didn't want either one of them to think I was sweating whatever they had steaming. I was immune.

"We should talk about this later," I suggested. I saw Randal standing off in a distance with her arms crossed.

"I don't wanna talk about this later, ER."

"Well, that's what I'm going to do."

"Oh, so you're trying to walk away from me now, is that it?" Jillian asked.

"You heard him. He's through," Randal added. I didn't notice her listening in.

The two of them had some tension up that had nothing to do with me. I was just tired of faking it with Jillian, and if ending it with her in public was what I needed to do to get her to leave me alone, then that was the route I was going to take. I had too much on my plate as it was, and I need to lighten it before everything spilled over.

My dad was tripping. My mom was trying to ease back into my life, and I had no idea what that was about. I now had the starting kicker role, and I didn't want to fail at it like I did the first time out. And I was starting to feel something for a girl other than my girlfriend. Seeing Gage standing back there with a smirk on his face let me know that, yeah, I needed to cut things off with Jillian before I ended up doing things that were illegal to set him straight. She was a liability to me, not an asset. Though she was acting like I was breaking her heart, for me it was just the opposite. Knowing she and I were over was cool because I was able to diminish pressure.

CHAPTER 3

Anxious Time

I turned to leave, but Jillian marched over to me and grabbed my arm. "ER, no, please don't break up with me. Please, not here. Please," she begged.

I just wanted to walk away, be left alone, and not have to deal with her whining, but that wasn't the type of guy I was. Although I was dealing with lots of issues, I was still a gentleman, even when I didn't want to be. I turned around.

Exhaling slowly, I whispered to her, "Why are you embarrassing yourself?"

"Because I love you and I don't want this to be over, okay? All right, I made some mistakes, but can we talk about them? You don't have to drop me like some class you don't want to take anymore."

My boys were watching the scene. I scratched my head, not knowing what to do. Amir called me over.

He said, "Look, I ain't trying to get in your business."

"Nah, man, say what you gotta say."

"All right, here it is," Amir observed. "I had a girl who really liked me. She was going extra crazy, freaking out on me, and following me all over the place. She tried to kill herself when I just went cold turkey on her. I'm not saying you need to be with a nut, but take the girl home and talk to her, man. I still feel bad about how things played out with the girl who stalked me. So I'm telling you from experience, I don't want you to be in the same boat. You know what I'm saying, ER?"

"I hear you, man. I appreciate that a lot. I didn't drive, though," I said. The rest of my friends came around Amir and me.

"Well, she's probably still got to perform. I got time to run you back to the school to get your car. The girls are going to lunch, so I don't have to wait on Hallie. You can come back to pick her up," Amir said, having an answer for everything.

But he was surely right about one thing: I would not be able to take it if something crazy happened because of me. I went back over to Jillian, reached out for her hand, and pulled her close. She was really emotional.

I whispered, "I'm going to get my car. After your performance we can talk, okay? Don't cry."

"Thank you, ER. I love you."

"All right, I'll see you in a few. I should be back in thirty minutes."

"Okay, perfect."

It was perfect for her, but it wasn't perfect for me. I meant it when I said I wanted to break up. Now I was setting myself up for another round of misery.

About an hour later, I was driving Jillian home. The eerie ride was a little unsettling. I could see she wanted so much from me. She was breathing heavily, fluttering her eyes my way, and was fidgety. My problem was I couldn't make my heart do what it didn't want to do. I cared for her, but not in the way I used to. I didn't know if not going to the same school with her was the difference, but I knew absence did not make the heart grow fonder. At Lockwood, I'd been watching people live and express themselves out loud and not always be so uptight and quiet because that was what was expected.

As we pulled into her empty driveway, Jillian said, "I'm sorry I pressured you, ER. Please come in. Let's talk."

"No, I'd rather talk right here."

I wanted to say there was nothing to say since we hadn't talked for the last thirty minutes. However, I knew we were both contemplating what was next and probably wanted to avoid this tough conversation. Inevitably, it was time for it to be had.

"Why did you break up with me? You're my heart, ER. You sent me in a state of panic when you broke things off earlier. Don't get me wrong, I'm so grateful to be able to have this opportunity to tell you that I actually want another chance. Last night, did I upset you wanting to take our relationship up another notch?"

"No. Yes. I don't know," I waffled, trying not to own up to what I was really feeling, but knowing deep within that I needed to. "I wanted things to be right. I didn't want to do it in the car, and you didn't respect that. So yeah, that did upset me. It's just a lot of things, Jillian. I think that we are growing apart."

Before I could finish my thoughts, she leaned over and kissed me deeply. While I might not have been connecting with her emotionally, my loins sure were in sync with everything she wanted me to feel. Problem was, how did I separate my desire from my sense of right and wrong?

I didn't ask her to start making me feel good, but that's what was happening. At that point, I didn't really care about doing the right thing. Though deep down I didn't want to be with Jillian, at that moment I didn't want her to stop. I kissed her hard and she started panting.

She cried out, "ER, make me feel like a prized princess, please. I want you. I need you. I love you."

Hearing her crave me, I panicked. I kept what was in my pants securely there. I pulled back over to the driver's side of the car and sighed.

Trying to be sensitive, I said lightly, "I can't."

Immediately, she went off. "Why can't you be like Gage? Why do you have to do this? Why don't you want me like he does?"

"Get out, Jillian. You're home. Just get out," I shouted. I was sick and tired of listening to her criticize me and put me down.

"No, no, no. I'm sorry," she started whining again.

"You don't have to be sorry, Jillian. You want more than I'm willing to give."

"And why? Don't you like this?" she said. She lifted her shirt and opened her bra.

A part of me wanted to bury my head in her chest, but instead, I just looked out of the driver's side window shaking my head. What in the world was wrong with me? Most boys my age would hit it, go, and not care about anyone's feelings. I should just tell her everything that she wanted to hear to get my fix on. Why wasn't I like that? Why did it not feel right to give her all that she was asking for to show her that Gage had nothing on me? Why did it not feel right to take her inside her empty house and sex her down?

As Jillian felt embarrassed and fixed her clothes, she said, "Is it so bad that I love you?"

"But why? Why do you think you love me?"

"I don't think I love you, ER. I know I do. I miss seeing you in the hallways. I long to say hello to you in the morning. I want to put my lips on yours. Being around you makes me a better person. I want you to be proud of me. I know I'm a little pushy in my tactics. I know I'm spoiled, but I want to change for you. If that's not love, then what is? I know deep down you love me too."

I didn't have the heart to tell her that I didn't love her. There was no way I could bring myself to actually tell her that she'd been making me sick. She reached in her purse and pulled out a condom.

"I have this if you're worried about me getting pregnant or anything."

My mind started racing. Why does my girlfriend have a condom in her purse? I saw the way Gage was looking at her and then looking at me like, *Ha-ha, just so you know, I got that. I hit that, partner. There!* When in reality, I knew he wasn't my partner at all, but I didn't want to ask the tough question. I did not want to know if they were intimate or not.

"Can't we just try to keep this going? Don't you want me to still be your girlfriend? Can't you tell me we're gonna be okay?"

"Don't cry," I said.

Though I didn't give her reason to, Jillian was really into me. I had to think of another way to break things off. Maybe I could sleep on it to see if I could feel something real for her again. Our relationship had been status quo for so long. She deserved all of me or none of me. Our in-between status was ruining us both.

"Let's keep trying," I said to her. "We'll both get what we want. No worries."

She leaned over, kissed me on the cheek, and got out of the car. Jillian waved and blew kisses. As I drove away, I was worried and wondered if I had made the right decision by extending things. In my gut, I felt I had not.

"What the heck, man? You better get out of my face!" Blake yelled to Waxton. "You talking all that noise about what I can and can't do. You need make sure you bring it on Friday night."

"Don't get sensitive like a little baby or a doggone little girl when I'm calling you out. Let's see the facts. Who had four interceptions in the last two games? Blake Strong. Who's completion percentage is close to thirty percent? Blake Strong. Who's been overthrowing all his receivers, tight ends, and running backs? Blake Doggone Strong," Waxton seethed and gave Blake a hard shove.

Blake was so irritated. While his game had been a little off, he still delivered when we needed it. In addition to drama he had with his mom's illness, he recently had a car accident. Word was he was hitting the bottle a little too much.

"Who's our weakest link on the team?" Waxton asked.

A bunch of football players, who were underclassmen and loved being Waxton's pets, yelled out, "Blake Strong."

"Please, you scrubs don't know what y'all are talking about," Blake hissed.

Landon immediately went over to him and said, "Man, just settle down. You know he just talking junk."

"Get your hand off of me," Blake said to Landon. "He can be the quarterback if he thinks he can do better."

"So what you gonna do? Just quit like a lil' bee-yotch?" Wax taunted.

"Oh heck nah," Blake said, trying to punch Waxton in the face.

Wax would not let that happen. He jumped around as if he was in a boxing ring, just sort of playing and toying with Blake. Guys started throwing out money, like they were laying down bets. Tons of profanity was being thrown out. I had no idea where the coaches were, but whatever they were doing out there on the field, or in meetings, or with the principal, needed to be cut short because havoc was being wreaked in our locker room. This was a time for camaraderie, and it seemed like the players were losing their minds. It was Blake, Amir, Leo, and Landon against Wax and his cronies. Basically, the top players were going up against each other, flexing muscles and acting all big and bad.

Finally, I just screamed out, "Why you guys acting like thugs? Aren't we on the same team in here? All of our pent-up frustration and anger needs to be saved for Friday night. I just saw the Giants play and they aren't chumps."

"You stay out of this, white boy," Brick Bailey yelled. It looked like a whole bunch of other players agreed with him.

At that moment, I picked up a nearby trash can and tossed it across the room. "Listen, Brick, I'm tired of being called *white boy*."

Brick scoffed, "What you gonna do? Lie out and get a tan? Even if you do get a tan, you still gonna be white as snow. Ain't nobody in here feeling sorry for you being bummed out 'cause you have to deal with us calling you white."

"For real," Waxton added, giving Brick dap. "Let me school you, Stone. Every time I go to get a job application, they look at me crazy 'cause I'm black. I walk down the mall, security guards follow me like I'm trying to steal something. Can't even walk down the street without ladies looking at me thinking I want to take their purse, all because I'm black. I can't do nothing about it, and you sure as heck can't do nothing about us talking about your white tail up at our black school. If you don't like it, you should go back to where you came from."

"What the heck does color have to do with it?" Leo yelled. "This man has been in the trenches with us. And, Brick, keeping it real, no kicker is a hundred percent accurate, but look in the mirror before you start to accuse somebody. Did you kick even one percent through the uprights this year?"

Brick got offended and shouted, "Leo, man, this has nothing to do with you. But since you want to get all in it, ever since you got your nose up that girl's butt, you been soft as heck on the line."

Waxton tag teamed and uttered, "And from what I hear, D1 schools are laying off of you because they think you ain't bringing it."

"More like a cowardly lion," Brick said under his breath.

"Why don't you come over here and get a piece of it then?" Leo threatened.

"Or come get a piece of this white boy," I said, ticked and ready to smash the jerks. "That's who you really want to fight."

"Darn right, I should've bashed your head in for—"

"Okay, okay, what in the world is going on in here?" Coach Strong and the rest of the coaches finally arrived. "We leave for just a little while and y'all lose your minds."

Though Coach Strong was in there, the team was still going at each other pretty hard. I was really sick of the trash talking, name calling, and object throwing.

"We had unity, Coach, until he came," Brick said, pointing at me.

The harsh looks being thrown my way were completely unnecessary and unwarranted. I wasn't going to take it anymore. Yeah, the Lions had a great reputation among the top-school recruiters, and the class that I was in was being called the best class in the state. However, if I had to get talked down to, verbally stepped on, and abused, then they could have it and go back to Brick being their kicker. And good luck with that being successful.

"I'm out, Coach. I'm done with this," I said. "Since I'm the problem, since y'all want to point fingers at me, cool."

I headed toward the door. I didn't even get out of the door before the defensive coordinator, and the only white coach on the staff, came over to me and pulled my jersey. He motioned for me to follow him out of the room.

"Okay, what is wrong with you?" Coach Grey asked when we were outside.

"I just don't want to be here anymore, okay? This was just a bad choice. I'm going back to live with my mom."

"And as long as it took you to get eligible, you think it's that easy? You think you can just walk away? We're sitting here at the end of the season, ready for the playoffs. You're the man. Teams have been calling about you."

"Coach, please don't play me. Don't try to psych my mind up. You can stay here with these guys, who are acting like anim—shoot," I said, catching myself verbalizing my true insensitive thoughts. "Please don't tell them I said that or they'll go off on me even more. Coach, sometimes this place is a zoo, and I'm tired of it. I know what you're saying. I want to like it here at Lockwood, but let's be honest, there's a whole lot wrong at this school."

"You came from Grovehill. You think it's perfect over there? We got kids on drugs here, and they for sure got some addicts over there. Just because it's not in the news doesn't mean it's not happening everywhere. You and I both know that individuals can dress up suburban schools and make it look like everything is fine. Especially when they make it seem like they are unaffected by what they think are urban problems."

I did a double take when Coach said that to me. Both of us were white, but it caught me off guard that he was being so transparent with me and keeping it real like that. I scratched my head, not knowing how to respond.

"What? Don't look shocked. You wanna talk, let's talk. You get to see how it feels being a minority for a change. A lot of these kids are angry because they have to deal with problems that most of the kids over at Grovehill never have to go through. There are a lot more poor folks and broken families here."

"Yeah, so? What kind of excuse is that, Coach? My family is broken and poor, but I'm not trying to fight every five minutes. I've got in more fights in the last few weeks being at this school than I ever have in my whole life. Guys here make you have to prove your manhood with physical violence. To survive, I have to change. I'm angry. I'm frustrated. I feel too much pressure. It's like I'm on crack or going through a withdrawal or something. I never even touched the stuff, nor do I have a desire to, but it just seems like being here is pulling me down."

"Only you can answer that question. You have to look at what you have to offer as well as what can be offered to you. Why don't you man up now and start making the world a better place? What's running gonna do?" Coach asked. "So what if you need to stand up to a couple of these big-mouth guys and put them in their place? They might need a gut check. Just like you said, life is hard for everybody right now, so let's not condemn anybody unless we walk in their shoes. You'll be the minority here for another eighteen months; they'll be a minority all their lives."

"So you tolerate the bad behavior out of pity, Coach?"

"No, I'm just committed to helping those who want to be helped. We all got flaws, son, but walking away is just as bad as not giving it your all on the field. Football has no place for either type of quitter. Take the rest of the day off. I'll talk to Coach. If I see you tomorrow, we won't speak about this. If I don't see you, I know what path you chose. Just remember, the easy way out usually brings no reward. The most difficult accomplishments are often the most rewarding," Coach Grey mused. Then he hit my back and walked into the zoo with the Lions.

"Okay, so didn't I just break up the two of you guys earlier? This is ridiculous," Dr. Sapp preached.

When Wax charged at me right before seventh period, I remembered what Coach Grey said and let him have it. He needed to be taught a lesson. Wax was whining about his nose being broken. I had a cut over my lip, but I could take the pain. He talked all that junk about being tough, but why couldn't he act it?

"I can't afford to get suspended," Wax complained. He paced Dr. Sapp's office after the principal left the two of us in there alone—not a smart idea since we were there for fighting.

Even the PhD was doing reckless stuff. What a place … I hated Lockwood.

Wax kept babbling. "This is all your fault, man. If I get suspended and can't play in the game and ruin my one opportunity to show recruiters what I can do …"

I tuned the jerk out. Waxton was fast, and he definitely had a great season, but he had two problems: He was short. He didn't have the height D1 schools were looking for. He also didn't have the grades, which was another crazy thing I didn't understand. Why did black guys with great athletic talent cancel themselves out of going to college because their grades sucked? I heard stories about some of them being passed on in spite of their abilities on the court or the field. Didn't they wanna learn something? Without knowledge, how did they plan to make it in life?

The night before, I thought a lot about what Coach Grey said: that I shouldn't condemn anyone until I walked in their shoes. While I was the minority for only a season, it did not feel comfortable. I was not black, and I certainly did not know how that felt. But I made the decision to stay. I even planned to talk to my dad about all the frustration I was feeling, but I was not a quitter or a punk.

Dr. Sapp's office door opened and in walked our principal and two adults: a lady who appeared to be hot under the collar, and my father. The way Wax stood to his feet, I knew the lady was his mom. Hairs on my neck stood up too.

"Waxton, I had to leave my job to come up here to see about yourself fighting somebody," she lectured. Then she walked over to him and whacked him upside the head.

"Ouch, Mom. My head already hurts."

"Good," she said, popping him again.

"Now I see why I had to come up here. You fighting a white boy?" she mock-whispered. "You know the principal wasn't gonna let that go. Dang stupid!"

"Actually, ma'am, the two of these young men were fighting earlier in the day, and I did let it go," Dr. Sapp said, quickly letting her know he wasn't playing the race card.

"Sir, no disrespect, but did you actually catch us?" Waxton asked.

I didn't even want to look up. I didn't want to see my dad's face. I knew he was pissed.

"Just because your daddy owns the biggest nightclub in town doesn't mean we have college money. All these college folks saying they coming to this game, and now you might get suspended and can't play? Are you stupid?" she roared.

"If you got a real job instead of playing hostess every night, maybe you'd have money to send me to college."

"What did you say, boy?" she asked.

"Okay, y'all. Settle down now," Dr. Sapp ordered. He stepped between mother and son.

"I'm not gonna come in here and have my son disrespecting me. I work hard at that nightclub, and it keeps a roof over our heads. What was this all about anyway? Why you got beef with this boy?" Wax's mom asked.

"He tryna talk to my girl. You know I can't have that," Wax answered.

"You're a liar," I said, truly hot under the collar.

"ER," my dad gasped.

"No, Dad. He's lying!"

"Well, I'm sure he is. There's no way you'd want his girlfriend, right?"

"Yeah, answer your pops. There's no way you'd want my girlfriend—my black, the-darker-the-berry-the-sweeter-the-juice girlfriend."

"Dad, don't come in here sounding preju-diced," I requested.

My father argued, "You need to watch your mouth and don't tell me how to speak. If you would have come to school and did what you needed to do instead of chasing some girl who's just trying to throw herself on everybody in the school—"

I cut him off and said, "You don't even know Randal, Dad. What are you talking about?"

"So you're admitting you like his girlfriend," my dad said.

"She's not his girlfriend, okay?"

Wax butted in, "I had my eye on her. We had a thing that was about to get started—"

"Exactly. In your mind, something was about to pop off. You were disrespecting her," I countered.

"Dr. Sapp, could I speak to my son alone?" my father asked.

"Sure. Yeah," Dr. Sapp uttered. He was clear-ly taken aback at the whole weird exchange.

My dad opened the principal's office door. We stepped across the hall into the empty assistant principal's space. My dad pushed the door closed.

"What is wrong with you? Have you lost your mind? You didn't come over here to follow any of these fast-tail girls."

"But I'm a guy, Dad."

"Yeah, but I mean … Yeah, definitely, I want you to be in a relationship with a girl, but you got one. That Jill girl, shucks. You just saw her. Didn't y'all do all you needed to do to get yourself through the week? One of *these* girls here could end up pregnant. That's all they do."

"Dad, listen to yourself and how you sound! Plus, Randal is not … black."

"Oh, she's a white girl? I mean, most of the girls here that are white are sort of trashy—"

"Okay, Dad. Please. You're really scaring me right now because I didn't realize you were such a bigot."

"What do you mean?"

"You try to teach me not to be prejudiced and judgmental, but when you find out I'm dating someone who's not one hundred percent white, you freak out. You were married to a Caucasian lady, and uh, how'd that work out for you?"

"So you're admitting the girl isn't white?" he asked. Disgusted, I did not respond. He softened,

"All I'm saying is that you got a girlfriend, and if this Randal is dating someone else—"

"She isn't, Dad. He was coming on to her. He was rude and crude. I just stepped in. You taught me to be a man, and that's what I was doing."

"Yeah, be smart and go get some help from a teacher or something. Don't put yourself in harm's way, end up getting kicked out of the school, and blow everything we've worked for. I didn't move you clear across the city for you to be a nobody in a school like this. We're on the brink of basketball season here, son. You guys are on your way to the football playoffs, and you just want to blow all that? That boy's mom is right. I've seen him play; he's that running back. He's got a whole bunch of potential. And the two of y'all are just being stupid."

"Tensions are high around here. What can I say?"

"You need to get it fixed. Go in there and apologize to that principal so your butt doesn't get torn up by me when we get home."

I looked at my dad eye to eye, like, *I dare you to try and hit me. I dare you to try and touch me.*

I'm a man just like you, but he didn't flinch. So I opened up the door and went out to speak to Dr. Sapp, who was in the hallway.

"Sir, I just wanted to say—"

"It's cool, man. I understand. I just got done telling Wax that I had to call your parents because I've been giving you athletes too many passes. I need all the nonsense to stop for real, for real. This is a warning. I know you guys are nervous, but we need all the players on the field. Together we're going to make it through. Nobody's in trouble today 'cause I understand this is an anxious time."

CHAPTER 4

Foolish Behavior

Last week was my first time playing as a Lockwood Lion. Though I pulled it out, it wasn't a flawless performance. Driving up with my team to play my old school, Grovehill High, I wasn't all the way confident.

When we got to the school, it was even more packed than when I came before as a spectator. The game was being televised, and Grovehill needed to win this game to secure home-field advantage throughout their playoffs. Wasn't that something? Coach Strong had all of us ready to deny them. As we were parking the team bus, players were beating on the seats, rapping, joking, laughing, and fidgeting.

Coach Strong finally got fed up with our lack of concentration, stood up, and said, "Are y'all idiots or what? We got a big game to play in there tonight. Don't y'all see all these people out here? They're either here to cheer you on or to see you go down. We're ranked number one in our division, and some people want to see you fall. Don't help them. Concentrate."

We had a mix-up with the buses. They were late getting to Lockwood, thus making us late getting to Grovehill's stadium. When we arrived, we had to move at an accelerated pace; the kick-off was fast approaching.

"Tonight we're gonna stay on our game," Coach commanded. He gave an inspirational charge before we went out on the field. "We're playing the Giants, and they're sneaky beasts. You will be going about your business, and they will stomp down and crush you. Let's not do nothing crazy tonight. We don't need to show-boat. I'm aware that there are lots of scouts out there, but if we play our game, we will give them something impressive without all the antics. All hands in. All hearts strong. All minds ready. On three: one, two, three … Lions!"

"Lions!" we all shouted as we ran out onto the field ready to take down the Giants.

Coach Strong had us so charged up that I forgot my gloves. Though I was a kicker and I wasn't handling the ball, I wore them so my body temperature would be controlled. I needed to concentrate on the task at hand instead of freezing. Coach just told me to hurry up so I could get out there and warm up.

I was stunned when I went back into the locker room and saw Wax with a needle in his hand. I couldn't tell if he was shooting up steroids or speed. Either way he had something in his arm that wasn't supposed to be there. Just my luck, I had to be the one who came back here and caught him. It would have been so much easier to mind my own business, just turn around, go out, and act like I'd never seen it and let whatever was going to happen to him, happen.

As I backed up to leave the locker room, I ran into a metal trash can. Of course, that made a whole bunch of noise. Wax automatically looked up, and I didn't have enough time to hide. A part of me didn't want to. Somebody had to check his behind.

"You!" Waxton called out. "What? You spying on me?"

"Okay, dude, now you're paranoid," I said. "I came to pick up something I left behind."

"Yeah right," he said, like I was lying.

"The better question is, what are you in here doing, man?" I asked, caring when I had no reason at all to do so.

"Just mind your own business."

"Trust me, that's what I'm trying to do, but you're my teammate."

"Isn't this the school you came from? Maybe you need to go to the other team's locker room and put on their uniform and play against us," Wax said, making no sense.

"Maybe you need to stop avoiding the question by trying to get me upset and all. What are you doing? Are you taking steroids or something else? You're all fired up like a stick of dynamite ready to go off," I said, trying to see what it was, but I didn't even know what I was looking at.

"What are you talking about? And what needle? What bag?" Wax uttered. He shoved things into a locker.

"I'm not an idiot," I said to him.

"You don't understand, man. There's a lot of pressure out here. Blake, Leo, them cats just naturally talented, and they're not even seniors and got scouts looking at 'em. Tonight I need them looking at me. I'm the senior on this team with promise. Scouts been saying I've gone under the radar just a little this year. If I don't do something dynamic, they won't want me. You can't mess up my chance."

"Man, you've just taken an illegal something. You can go out there and have a heart attack or whatever," I lectured. Wax looked at me like I was a liar. "Come on, man. Whatever you got there was not prescribed by a doctor."

"How do you know?"

"Okay, so you admit you're taking something?"

"I didn't say that," Wax said. "I know I said some stuff to you in the past that's been a little judgmental. I know I give you a hard time, but I just need you to look the other way on this. Whatever I do to my body is on me. I just need a little boost. It's nothing serious. I'm not gonna do it anymore, all right? Dang, you can have your lil' kicks with Randal. I'll leave her alone. I don't want her anyway. I did wanna knock her boots, but I'll back off that, if you back off this."

"She and I are not an item anyway, Wax. Is a girl why you've been acting so crazy?"

"What are you talking about? Just keep your mouth closed, all right, punk?" Wax closed up his locker and made sure the lock was secured. Then he pushed me in the chest real hard and walked out.

Rationalizing that it was none of my business, I grabbed my gloves and went out of the locker room too. Just as I was thinking about if I should talk to Coach about what I just saw, I was coming out of Grovehill's tunnel and spotted Jillian and Gage in a lip-lock. I couldn't believe it. She was just begging me to work things out, assuring me that she wanted me, and then I catch her going hot and heavy with some other guy.

I got closer and yelled, "Boo!"

I scared the two of them. Jillian's eyes got wide. Gage held the familiar smirk I was used to seeing him give me lately.

Jillian tried to cover her tracks, "ER, I thought you were out there on the football field. I saw you earlier and you were—"

I was tired of playing games, so I snapped, "Yeah, I was, but I left something. Why am I explaining any of this to you? I was where I was supposed to be, but it seems like you were where you wanted to be."

"Yeah, and what's the problem with it? She told me you got something limp down there that won't get up like a man can," Gage taunted.

"*What?*" I was ready to throw a punch. I had already been used to fighting in the last few weeks. Hitting him would be a pleasure. The true punk stepped back and hid behind Jillian.

"Go ahead, Gage, hide like a little girl. The two of y'all deserve each other. You want me to be hard?" I demanded as I looked at Jillian. "We're through."

"ER, no!"

This time I was not going to be crazy. This time I was not going to be stupid. This time I wasn't going to fall for her pleading. With my helmet in one hand and my gloves in the other, I jogged onto the field and never looked back. Jillian and I were over, and no matter what, I'd never be stupid and fall for her again. Sad thing was, I knew Gage would jerk her around, but that wasn't my problem. I needed to go win a game. I heard her call out for me, but I wasn't moved. The only thing I was focused on was winning the game, not consoling a fool.

"We're kicking these white boys' tails," Waxton came to the sidelines and yelled after he scored the touchdown against Grovehill.

His comment fueled the fire. Yes, a few idiot fans from the home team had been shouting out racial slurs throughout the night, but we were supposed to be bigger than that. We were winning. Of course the opposing team's fans would be derogatory, but I was disappointed in our coaches. Coach Strong was so focused on winning that he didn't care if the character of his team was going out the window. I just had a funny feeling that all of the heated behavior that was brewing on the sidelines was going to blow up in our team's face.

I went over to Coach Grey and said, "Aren't y'all gonna do something? Cracker, trailer trash, skully, and a whole bunch of other racial slurs that I've never heard before tonight from our team can't be appropriate, Coach Grey."

"Son, don't be so sensitive. We're about to win this football game and be undefeated. I'm trying to get a head coaching job next year. Maybe I'll be able to come here and coach. Don't sweat the small stuff," Coach Grey responded and patted my helmet condescendingly.

"So you think this is right? You wouldn't tolerate the other team out there using the *N*-word."

He just shook his head, put on his headsets, and tried ignoring me. I kept watching him, and he looked back at me a couple times. He knew what I was saying had merit.

When the game was over, I jogged on the field to shake my old teammates' hands. They weren't happy they lost, but the guys were cordial. I was about to head to the locker room when I was abruptly stopped.

Gage came up to me and said, "Man, I don't get how you could even *like* playing with those animals."

I couldn't get too mad at Gage saying what he did. First of all, the guys I knew and admired all semester weren't acting like that. Wax and some of his crew were acting like the babies they had been all week. As Gage was going off on their ignorance, Waxton heard him and pushed him so hard that Gage fell. Guys from both teams asked no questions, they just started shoving each other. Shoving turned to pushing, and the pushing turned to punching. Soon, we had an all-out brawl. I looked over at Blake, Amir, Landon, and Leo, and they were fighting too. They had the nerve to look over at me like, *Why aren't you joining us?* But I wasn't gonna act like I was in a zoo.

"Come on, ER. Help us, man," Landon called.

"Right, dude, we're a team. You're either with us or against us," Leo hollered while throwing punches.

"I'm not gonna be a part of this," I said to them with a face that showed I was insulted by the request.

I just had a great game. I hit everything perfectly. I kicked the ball so far that I sent the other team deep every time. The cameras were rolling on this insane scene. Both sets of coaches, the police, and some administrators rushed to the brawl on the field. It took about twenty minutes to break up the scuffle, which was an embarrassment for both schools. Listening to reporters talk about the disgusting scene, I wasn't the only one who thought so. One reporter covering the story made a big deal about how ashamed everyone involved should be.

As I walked to the locker room, I felt I was walking alone, even though many guys were stampeding off in the same direction. I didn't fight with my old or new friends, but I didn't break up any fights either.

Gage abruptly brushed by me and said, "Not only are you not a lover, but you're not a fighter either, huh?"

"Shut up," I told him.

"Glad you left Grovehill," Gage uttered.

"Please, you wouldn't stand up with us. You should have stayed at Grovehill," Brick said. "We don't want you at Lockwood."

Most of the big-shot talkers got on the first bus. The underclassmen were on the second bus. That's the bus I went to.

Before I could get on it, Blake tugged on my jersey. "You were just standing there, man. Can you explain that to me? We were in a war, and you were just standing there."

"Those guys were my teammates. We were here to play football, not fight."

"So did you hear what they were saying about us?"

"You know I heard what y'all were saying all game about them, especially Wax," I said.

"Hey, man, no need in trying to talk to him," Waxton said to Blake. "Let the scrub get on the lil' boys bus, 'cause when it was time to put up, he shut up. Shoot, he shut down. Now we need to shut him out."

I just threw my hands up. He needed to be worrying about whatever substance he was putting in his body. He was the ringleader who started things getting out of control.

However, I got on the bus. I didn't even want to sit with any of the guys, so I kept going to the back. I was pleasantly surprised when I saw Randal Raines sitting in the back seat. My feet, knowing what my heart wanted, walked up to her.

"Is it okay if I sit with you?" I asked. We locked eyes—magic.

She paused. I knew she was probably questioning my motives. I was about to turn around and find another seat until the cheer coach told everyone to sit so the bus could leave. Randal slid over. I sat and took in her luscious smell. She calmed me.

"Congrats on the game," she opened up and said.

"Thanks," I said in a dull tone, thinking about the fight.

"Now on to the big game," Randal went on. It was then that I realized the cheerleaders probably didn't even see the brawl.

"You're right. Playoff time is here."

She volunteered, "It had to be awesome, kicking the ball through the uprights."

I smiled and asked, "Do you like football?"

"I do. My dad and brother love it, though my brother's at UGA on a baseball scholarship."

"Wow, I didn't know that."

"You did really good," she said with sparkling eyes.

I thought she was so beautiful. She was giving me a compliment, but I wanted to give her one. However, I didn't want to scare her away. I leaned my head against the back window. I had so much on my mind. I wanted to open up to her, but I figured now wasn't the right time. However, she talked and made me feel better.

When we pulled up to Lockwood, I dreaded getting off the bus. I enjoyed sitting beside Randal, and I would have been fine with doing that all night. Talking to her was so relaxing, and not dealing with reality while around her was like a dream come true. I'm not saying that I felt like prince charming around her, but there was definitely something magical happening. I was honestly tired of fighting my feelings. Jillian did me a favor by kissing Gage. Luck was my best friend by allowing me to witness her betrayal.

Walking off the bus, I saw the guys. Many sets of eyes rolled my way. Regardless of whether or not the Giants or Lions thought I had balls, I knew it took a man to resist taking sides when I felt both were wrong.

I got off the bus before Randal. Immediately, I turned and held out my hand to assist her down. Holding her dainty hand, I felt that soon I'd have to tell her that I liked her so we could explore the possibilities.

"Good night," I said, wanting to hug her.

"Don't let all the stuff stress you," she replied. I smiled. "Here's your phone. It was on the seat. I just put my number in. Call me if you ever want football tips. I really want to thank you for standing up to Wax for me."

I nodded and then turned to face the guys. Landon and Leo came to me. They wouldn't move, like they wanted to intimidate me or something.

"Y'all wanna go talk or what?" I said, knowing we needed to address the tension.

"We just thought you were our boy. That's all, ER," Leo said coldly.

Landon agreed, "We just need an explanation for why you left the team to fight without your help."

I said, "You know, sometimes you can only stand up when you know that what you're fighting for is right, not when you are being pressured. Shoot, Landon just went through the big molestation case. People had been on him to open up his mouth and testify. He had to face his own demons about wanting to reveal or not reveal his connection."

"What are you saying, ER?" Landon asked. "Are you saying that because I didn't wanna say anything back then—which was wrong on my part—you feel you didn't have to help us out when guys were jumping us?"

"There are so many guys on this team. You weren't unevenly matched, Landon. Don't overdramatize the situation. Besides, I was caught in the middle. You know I went to school with those guys."

"So it's okay for them to call us any ole word?" Leo asked.

"Did you hear anybody use the *N*-word, man? Straight up, seriously, or did you see Waxton getting his tail beat and you jumped in?" I asked, tired of the bull. "You guys have had my back since I've been in this school."

"Exactly! And all we were asking was for you to step up and be with us. You're on our team, ER. Your loyalties can't be split, man," Landon said, like I'd really let him down.

"But if I see y'all shooting up drugs, does that mean I'm supposed to roll up my sleeve and stick the needle in my arm too?" I asked, alluding to much more.

Both of them looked at me like I was crazy. They didn't know it, but I was trying to tell them Waxton was high. They were following his stupid moves not even understanding the full picture. I wasn't going to be a part of that, even if it meant losing their friendship.

"Man, you talking stupid," Leo said to me.

I tried not to get offended. He didn't call me stupid. He said what I said was stupid, even though he didn't understand where I was coming from. I took his little jab. I just threw my hand up and walked away. I got called a lot of other things from a lot of other players. I wanted to find Waxton and wring his neck. I knew he was probably somewhere getting another hit, but I couldn't dwell on that. I decided to let his business be his business, so there was absolutely no reason to worry if he wasted his life away. That would be his problem.

Coach Grey came over to me before I got in my car and said, "Listen, I owe you an apology."

"For what, Coach?"

"For not listening to you earlier. You tried to tell everybody to settle down, but I just thought it was good for the game, and now we could be disqualified from the playoffs for the fight. I can't say I wasn't warned. You couldn't stop all those guys from doing what they did, but you did keep on standing for what you knew was right. I saw you out there with guys wanting you to join the fight, and you didn't crumple to the pressure. Your actions were admirable. You're going somewhere, ER Stone. You're the kind of guy who helps us adults get it right. I thought you needed to know that."

"Thanks, Coach," I sighed. Then I got into my car and headed home.

The next day, I didn't wake up until the afternoon. I had the place to myself and I loved it. My dad was on his way back from a meeting at Walmart's headquarters in Bentonville, Arkansas. While he said he trusted me, the leash he had me on was very short. He'd left a ton of messages. So had my mom. I texted them both to let them know I was fine.

Instead of staying home by myself all evening, I decided to go to my mom's place so we could talk. Plus, I wanted a good meal. I really wanted to talk to her about the football fight as well. She was so open-minded, and she saw the good in every situation. I thought if I talked to her, she could make some sense of my woes. Honestly, I didn't want Landon and the guys to hate me, but wasn't I right? She was my mom, and talking was something we hadn't done in a long time. With her help, I knew I could get a better perspective on my situation.

Ever since I let my teammates know what I would and wouldn't put up with, they'd made me an outcast. Did I even belong at Lockwood? I thought I did. I'd come to terms with being the minority and I felt like I was fitting in.

I knew I didn't want to go back to Grovehill just because I blended in better. And something told me I didn't share the same beliefs as a lot of those guys.

I called to make sure it was okay to come, but the phone went straight to her voicemail. I had a key, so I just headed over. I was really tired when I pulled up. When I opened the door, the alarm didn't go off, which was odd because my mom always put it on.

Suddenly, I heard noises. It seemed kind of crazy for me to think I could go upstairs and be able to handle an intruder. However, instinct kicked in, and I couldn't let anyone steal from my mom. Though I wouldn't jump into a fight that I thought was pointless, I certainly would attack someone taking my mom's stuff.

She had a steel poker by the fireplace that I grabbed before heading upstairs. Knowing Landon was ticked at me, I realized he was the only one I knew who always checked his cell. It was like the thing was glued to his hip or something, so I pulled out my cell and texted real fast.

"I know we got issues, but straight up, I'm at my mom's place and I hear noises. If I don't hit you back in ten, send someone to 2364 Brentmoore Point."

Immediately he texted back, "Dude, be careful. Taking my lil' bro to a movie, but I'm there if you need me."

I texted back, "Thanks."

The noises were coming from my mom's bedroom. I opened the door, flicked on the lights, and yelled, "I got you!"

I was stunned to see my mom and a lady—who I didn't know—rolling around under the covers on my mom's bed. Their faces looked sweaty, and I think they were both naked.

I dropped the fireplace poker and stood looking in amazement. My mom was making out with a woman. I was so embarrassed. I had caught my mother in a very personal situation. I didn't know what to do or where to turn. This was so unexpected. I freaked out. I was tripping that my mom was engaging in such foolish behavior.

CHAPTER 5

Downright Disgusted

Mom, what is going on in here? Why are you with that woman? Mom, I don't understand!" I cried. What was she thinking?

"Oh my gosh, ER. Oh my gosh! Sorry," my mom cried.

She tossed on a T-shirt and rushed toward me. I was freaked, but seeing the other lady get out of the bed *really* did a number on my head. Watching two middle-aged women scramble around the bedroom after what I knew they had been doing really messed me up. I turned around immediately. I tried to make a quick escape, but my mom grabbed me before I could get through the door.

"Just let him go, Lydia," the other lady suggested mildly.

"Jane, please, this is my son. I can't just let him go," she argued.

"How could you, Mom?" I asked.

"How could she what? She's a grown woman. She hadn't done anything to you. Being gay isn't something she can just fix. It's not like she has a disease," Jane preached.

I shot her a hard look. She wouldn't dare think of saying anything else to me. I could tell that my mom was furious with her. Jane pushed past me and stormed out of the room.

My mom said, "I didn't know you were coming, ER. If I would have known, I certainly wouldn't of—"

"You certainly wouldn't have what? Been in the bed with some woman?"

"Please, watch how you talk to me. I am your mother."

"Are you sure? Because I didn't know *my* mom was a lesbian."

My mom had a bench at the end of her bed. I sat on it, put both of my hands on my head, and just rocked back and forth. She touched my shoulders, but I jerked away. It was a lot, but now so many things were starting to make sense. Now I understood why my dad didn't want me to live with her, and why she didn't want to fight for me—she wanted none of this exposed.

"Mom, why this lifestyle? Why a woman? I get you and dad needed to end things. You still got a lot of life in you, and you don't want to live alone, but couldn't you have found another guy?"

"I did find somebody else. This isn't just a fling. This isn't just something I'm trying. Jane is my partner."

"So that's why you let me leave, so she could live here with you?"

"Because I haven't told you, we haven't made that full commitment of living together, but I do stay over at her place some nights, and she stays here others." My mom started crying. "I didn't want you to find out like this."

All of this wasn't okay. I didn't want any explanations. I just knew there was nothing she could say to make me understand this ... this lifestyle she had chosen. It didn't just affect her; it touched my life too. I did not understand her choice at all.

"Please talk to me, ER. Please don't go, son." She reached over to hold my arm.

Pulling away, I said, "Mom, don't try to stop me."

"I love you, son. This doesn't change that."

Because I was so confused, it changed everything for me. My mom had told me their marriage didn't work because my dad had become too depressed with job changes, and his mood swings were intolerable. Now, I wasn't sure if that had been true at all. Did she leave out vital information?

When I tried to leave, Jane appeared in front of the door. "You're not leaving. You can't have your mom all upset like that. You need to turn on around, man up, and talk to her."

"I get that you're like the person who thinks they have the balls in this relationship you're in with my mom, but let's be clear, lady, you're not telling me what to do. Move!"

"Okay," she said and got out of my way.

When I got in my car, I *so* wanted to drive recklessly, but that wasn't my style. I wanted to go home and raid my dad's liquor cabinet, but I had no desire to drink. I wanted to find Waxton and shoot up whatever it was that he was shooting, but I knew that was wrong and crazy. But I had to do something wild and crazy.

I immediately thought about how Randal Raines had given me her digits. I hadn't been able to get her beautiful self out of my mind. She was in my thoughts. She was in my dreams, and I wanted her to be in my arms to help make this all go away. Talking to her, I could feel there was a connection. I didn't know if she'd hang up in my face, but I needed to find out.

I decided to be spontaneous and call Randal. Scrolling my phone, I searched for the entry that she said she made when I left my phone on the bus. I was relieved when I found it. I felt nervous when the phone rang. I was always calm and collected when it came to girls, but now I was sweating and contemplating hanging up.

I couldn't when I heard Randal's sweet voice say, "Hello?"

Mumbling, I said, "Randal, hi. It's ER. Can I talk to you for a second?"

She paused. I heard some noise in the background. I didn't know if she was distracted or if she didn't want to talk to me.

I did not have to guess what the issue was because she finally said, "ER Stone? Really? What do you want with me? Call Jillian!"

That was fair. I knew she knew I had a girl. However, she didn't know the latest.

I said, "Hold up. Jillian and I are through."

"So you think I'm a dummy? Sell that tired story to the tabloids. I know the truth. Miss Jillian confronted me at the state cheerleading competition. She told me how hot things are between you two. So bye, ER."

Needing to set the record straight, I said, "Randal, hold up! Let me explain!"

"Explain what?" she said, cutting me no slack.

Wanting to speak to her in person, I said, "I need to see you. I know I have no right to ask you last minute, but I'd like to pick you up and explain in person. Your home is close to Lockwood, right?"

She grumbled, "Wait, I didn't say I'd go out with you."

"You can't go anywhere! You have company," I heard a voice say.

Whoever it was, Randal wasn't feeling them. She hushed the person and then gave me her address. It took me no time to get over to her place.

As soon as I arrived at her door, she was waiting. She sort of rushed me out of the driveway. Not asking if she was okay, I just drove. Both of us were uneasy.

To make her comfortable I said, "Sorry I was so last minute."

"No biggie," she said. "What's up?"

"A bunch. Bottom line is, though, I wanted to be with you."

"Why not Jillian? I did just see her, and she rubbed it in my face about how great things were going with you guys."

"Some of the stuff that Jillian and I went through was personal. But make no mistake about it, we are over. I want to get to know you."

"Maybe now is too soon for you to be in another relationship. Not saying that's what you're saying," Randal went on, sort of embarrassed that she was being presumptuous.

Darn, she was making my heart flutter. I gave her hand a squeeze. We were both feeling something.

"I'm making you uncomfortable, huh?" I asked.

"A lot is going on with me right now, ER. And what does ER stand for anyway?"

"Edgar Remington Stone and I go by my initials for that reason, so hold on to the secret," I teased. "You're beautiful, Randal, on the inside and out. Lockwood is a crazy place. Most days I don't feel I fit in, but when I see your light, I want to be there. Not trying to freak you out, but that's just how I feel."

"I think you've given me more credit than I deserve," she admitted. And I saw pain in her eyes. "Right now my life is so crazy."

"Mine too. Maybe we can help each other get our lives sane," I suggested gently. I brushed her cheek, and her eyes rolled back in a way that I could tell she enjoyed the touch.

"Maybe we can."

I couldn't believe what had just happened. There I was having a great time with Randal, out on our first unofficial date. We were spending time together, and she seemed happy. Then out of nowhere she left with Becca! And though Becca and I had been at Grovehill together for the last two years, I didn't know her well, but I knew her well enough to know she liked girls. Noticing Becca being so forceful and protective over girls at my old school, I knew that was because she had ulterior motives behind her actions. For Randal to abruptly jet, was she into that too? I just started shaking my head before I could dive deeper into my analysis.

I was punched lightly in the back by Landon. "Hey, dude, I was just about to reach out to you. Your mom's okay then? You never texted me back, but you're here at the movies alone."

I apologized. "Too much swirling around in my head. I should have texted back."

"Wait, he's the kicker for the Lions," a mini version of Landon spoke out. "He could have come to the movies with us."

"Is this your brother?" I asked, extending my hand.

"Yeah, thanks for not saying his little brother," the kid said to me.

"That's 'cause he can see that," Landon teased. "Logan, this is the—"

"I know, I know. He's ER Stone. Just so you know," little Logan said to me, "all my friends have been trying to kick like you."

"What? I thought your friends wanted to be a wide receiver like me," Landon joked.

"Please. We looked up the lifespan of a kicker in the NFL, and they kick for years. Wide receivers come and go. He's the man."

His admiration made me smile. I suddenly hoped I lived up to the expectations of the little guys in the community. I remembered kicking with some of them when we had a football camp a few weeks back, but I never really thought I had any impact so that was great to hear.

"Uh, dude, I'll be right back. I gotta go to the bathroom," Logan said, trying to be extra cool to his brother.

"Straight there and right back," Landon instructed. "Dang, boy, you drink one Coke and you gotta pee a swimming pool."

"Ha-ha-ha," Logan said.

I could tell the two of them had a nice bond. A part of me wished I had a sibling, but as stubborn as my dad was and the way my mom was carrying on, I knew that would never happen. It looked like I didn't even have a chance at getting a half brother or sister. When Logan took off, I admired the way Landon watched him.

I admitted, "You're lucky to have him."

"Yeah, I really am. It took a tragedy for me to wake up and notice he was sitting right there needing my guidance. He thinks he's so cool."

"Trying to be like his big brother, that's all."

"Yeah, and I'm trying hard not to let him down, you know?"

"Yep, I do. So you guys still mad, huh?" I said, getting all of the hot air out of the way.

"Can you talk to me, man? Tell me what's been going on with you. Why you been so upset lately? Inside your mind, you really think all us black folks are crazy?" Landon asked.

"Honestly, maybe I did before I got to Lockwood, but being there, meeting folks like you, Leo, Blake, Amir, Brenton, and Coach Strong—"

"And Randal," Landon added.

"What are you talking about?"

"Waxton's baited you repeatedly. You don't just fight with him because you have no interest. I mean, you weren't just being chivalrous and all. Forget her for now, I want you to talk to me. You said you know I ain't some loose ghetto thug. Why then does it seem like you got all this hostility inside you?"

" 'Cause when I try not to see color, color is all around me. Some of y'all call me white boy—"

"I know, man, but that's also respect the way they say it. You saved our tails coming in being the kicker. Brick's just jealous, and Wax, he's been tripping lately—something else has been going on with him."

I looked away because I knew what that something else was, but I didn't want to go there. I wasn't trying to add tattletale to the list of titles I was already wearing. Wax did need to straighten up, though.

"You guys can call each other all kinds of names, but if I just speak my mind and say what I really think, I'm the most hated man at Lockwood."

Landon said, "Look, ER, all of us got haters out there. Some hate Blake 'cause his dad's the coach. Folks hate me 'cause they think my dad's got dough. Folks hate you 'cause of the color of your skin. I mean, shoot, we just have to live with it."

"Easy for you to say, Landon. You're not the one at school every day with people giving you the eye like they really want to take you to the back alley somewhere and beat you black and blue. I'm not saying all white people are right, but that doesn't mean I have to pay for their wrongs. I'm just a little tired of everything being amplified when it comes to me."

"What are you talking about?" Landon said, not understanding my world.

"On the football field, I'm the kicker, and I'm supposed to send the ball through the uprights. But come on, you just said it. Brick hadn't hit anything all year. I missed one, and I get all kinds of boos?"

"Yeah, but you know for a kicker it's timing, and that was first kick, so they're thinking you're more of the same. Why put a white boy in who's gonna mess up just like the black boy did? If that's the case, they might as well have kept Brick in. I know that's what everyone was thinking, but you showed them, and you shut them up. You showed them it wasn't about color; it was about skills when you hit all of the next three extra points. Don't get offended," Landon said. "I think what upset me is that we've been having your back. Just like you don't want to get lumped in with the crazy white people out there, we don't want to get lumped in with the crazy black thugs, especially not in the eyes of the guy who should know us."

"It's the end of the season, Landon. I would have thought we'd all be as one."

"I just couldn't believe you wouldn't fight with us after we stood up for you."

"I understand that."

"Your friends were wrong," Landon said.

"Yeah, but what I need you to understand is that no one was right."

For a moment, we held each other's gaze. We were both a little bummed we couldn't get where the other was coming from. He had his stance and I had mine. When his little brother came out, we went our separate ways. I hoped that we could get past it, but I wasn't sure.

My phone was blowing up, and it was ticking me off that my parents kept calling. I'm sure my mom got in touch with my father and told him what happened because both of them were calling as if they hadn't heard from me in days. However, I still wasn't ready to go home.

I was hungry, and I knew if my dad had made it home, he hadn't fixed anything to eat. So I pulled into Church's Chicken. I'd been there before with Leo and Landon and loved it. I had a craving for the good-tasting chicken.

I pulled around through the driveway and was stunned to see Waxton over by the dumpster handing some sketchy guy a wad of cash. In exchange he got a small baggie. I couldn't believe what I was seeing.

When I decided not to tell on Waxton before the game, I thought it was a one time thing. So I let it all go. I minded my own business. I stayed to myself, and I didn't get in his face about what he was doing. Now I was seriously upset with the jerk. I was sure it wasn't steroids he was getting in the middle of the night. Come to think of it, taking drugs would explain his erratic behavior, always causing a ruckus on the football team because he was unstable. And just like I had gotten in his grill because he had gone too far with Randal, I planned to park the car, get my food, and get in his face about using.

A part of me wondered why I even cared. All he was giving me was grief. Now I realized it wasn't really about Wax. Who knew how long he was on the stuff? It was evident he was pretty messed up, and I wanted to offer to help him, though I was sure he would refuse it. However, before I could confront him myself, my phone rang again. I looked down and was stunned to see Landon's number.

"What's up?" I said. I was hopeful he was calling to work things out.

"Dude, I heard what you said, and I just wanted to let you know we're straight. I understand you didn't want to get involved in all the nonsense. I can see that it was all nonsense. Coach said about as much. I had no business fighting those boys."

"I appreciate that, man," I said.

"But look, I need to talk to you in person. I got something I need you to handle for me."

"Huh?" I said, wanting more details.

"Um, have you eaten? Can you meet me at IHOP?"

"I'll be there in a little while."

"I wanted to talk. I knew you were out, so I was just trying to catch you," Landon added.

"Yeah, sure. No problem," I said, driving out of the Church's Chicken lot.

As hungry as I was, I tried not to eat anything as I waited for Landon in the restaurant. He asked me to grab some grub, so I didn't want to be rude. When he came inside the restaurant and told me Randal was outside, shaken, and really wanting to talk to me, I quickly got up and dashed out the door, forgetting all about eating and how hungry I was.

I called out, "Randal, you out here? Landon said you're out here to see me. Where are you?"

Eva, Landon's girl, was hugging Randal and she waved me over. "ER, we are over here. I'm Eva Blount."

"Nice to meet you. I'm ER Stone." We shook hands.

Eva squeezed my hand hard and pulled me toward her. "Look, white boy, let me be clear … you're a guy, and Randal is a cute girl, so I know what's on your mind. But think different thoughts 'cause it ain't happening. Randal is a nice girl … a really, really nice girl. You understand?"

"Ee-vah," Randal said, clearly embarrassed by her overprotective friend.

"Yes?" Eva responded with her eyebrows raised.

Randal shoved her buddy toward the restaurant. Eva kept eyeing me. I nodded, letting her know I got the message and would not cross any lines. I needed her to go so I could find out why Randal dissed me earlier. I wanted answers way more than my growling stomach wanted a meal.

I could not read Randal. She seemed too timid to address the obvious issue we needed to discuss. Before I could get to it, she pulled my head to hers and kissed me. For a long moment, I'd forgotten everything as I was so wrapped up in the strong connection. However, I realized her behavior was erratic. I didn't want her to have regrets. Why kiss if the air between us was polluted?

I stepped back and sternly said, "Wait, we need to talk. I deserve an explanation, not a sympathy kiss."

"It wasn't sympathy," Randal said.

"Then what?"

She started trembling. I asked her to come with me to my car so we could talk. She agreed.

After the both of us sat in my ride quietly for a long while, I asked, "Randal, we were having a great time then you dipped. Please talk to me. Did I do something?"

"No, of course not. It's just ... I don't even know where to start," Randal cried. I got that there was clearly something big bothering her.

"Just tell me why you were with Becca. She's—"

"Gay," Randal completed my thought, as I was struggling to say what I wanted to say. "You want to know? Here it goes. She's sleeping over."

I squinted, trying to figure out what exactly she was pushing to tell me. My eyes widened when Randal revealed Becca came on to her after they shared a joint, which she had tried for the first time.

"ER, right before you, I kissed a girl."

"And?" I asked, trying to see if she liked it.

"That's the thing that's bothering me. I'm not sure. I do know I have no desire to be in a relationship with a female. Same-sex couples are everywhere nowadays, but I don't want to be in one of them. So shoot me, but that's why I kissed you. I wanted to *feel* something."

"Did you?" I asked, as I knew her kiss had me rising.

"Yes," she responded, kissing my hand. "But hearing all that information probably alarms you, huh? You're having no luck with girls, because I know Jillian is crazy, and now I'm a little loony too. Don't know if I'm gay or straight, black or white, coming or going. I'm just all mixed up."

"None of us have it all together," I said, realizing I wasn't the only one under pressure.

"You really have it together, ER," Randal said, clearly giving me way more credit than I deserved.

"I want to tell you something that I'd like you to keep between us," I told her. She smiled in agreement. "My dad moved me abruptly a few months back. I didn't know why, and I didn't see it coming. All I knew was that he didn't want me to live with my mom. Well, tonight I go over to her place to talk, and I catch her in bed with a lady. I feel sick just talking about it. Sounds like you were trying something out of curiosity. That's not what she's doing. She's made a choice to live this way. How do you think I feel knowing my mom kept such a huge secret from me? I called you earlier tonight because I needed you."

She reached over and placed her arms around me. I held on tighter. She couldn't erase my woes, but in that embrace she made me feel ten times better. The look in her eyes told me she was there for me, and I did not have to be so downright disgusted.

CHAPTER 6
Certain Lane

Why don't you stop calling me already? I'll get home when I get there!" I yelled into the receiver, though I didn't answer the phone.

I wasn't crazy. It was my dad dialing me up again, and I hadn't listened to any of his messages. It was past one o'clock in the morning, and I had never been known to be out that late. I knew he was worried, but I had a life-altering experience. It's not every day a kid finds out his mom is gay.

While I knew he just wanted to talk to me about my feelings, I couldn't connect with him. Shoot, truth be told, I was angry at him. I didn't know how long he had known this, but I was certain that when he came in September and abruptly uprooted me from my mom's home, he knew. It explained everything that was mysterious about that time, except why he didn't tell me.

I wasn't a kid anymore, and my dad had left me in the dark about everything for months. He only wanted to talk to me now because hiding the truth was no longer an option. And to be fair, I'm sure he wanted to talk to me to make sure I was all right.

I had been the good son. I hadn't given them a lot of drama when they divorced. Yeah, I cried a little and pouted some, but I kept quiet. I wasn't over-the-top about it. I didn't turn to drugs, crash a car, or do anything stupid. No, I was their good boy. I had proven to them that I actually was a man.

Going home was inevitable. I knew my father was already upset that I hadn't responded to his calls. The last thing I wanted to do was send him into a state of panic by not coming in at all. Trying to be slick, I turned off my headlights when I pulled into the driveway. My dad's room was off the front of the house, and if he was asleep, I certainly didn't want to wake him. We could talk about all this in the morning. Nothing was going to change over the next few hours.

As soon as I reached for the front door, I realized my dad was not asleep. The door was open. When I stepped inside, he was sitting in his recliner with a grim look on his face.

"In the morning, Dad," I said. I threw up my hand and tried to walk past him, but he quickly stood to his feet, letting me know that though he didn't train daily like I did, he could still handle me if he had to.

"No, son, we're talking right now, so you might as well come on back to this family room and sit your butt down."

"I'm tired, though, Dad."

"I guess you are. Your watch break? You didn't think I'd be worried? You're too busy doing whatever to pick up the telephone and let me know you're okay? Your mother's worried sick, and honestly, I've been half out of my mind with worry about you."

I shrugged my shoulders. He didn't want me to respond to that. Big deal, the two of them had been worried. I felt so bad. *Not.* With the big secret the two of them had kept from me, like they had no concern for my feelings, I didn't care about theirs. I sat on the sofa, but I didn't say anything. I just looked at him. He wanted to talk now, and I told him I was tired. Clearly, he could see I had an attitude, so there was no need to play with each other. I was so passed that.

"So you are going to act like a brat? I've been worried all night. You're just gonna come in here acting all big and bad. Fine, you're too big for me to spank, so I'll just take your car keys."

I handed them over to him. I wanted to throw them, but I had respect. He looked surprised, but at that point, I really didn't care. The clock just needed to hurry up so I could get out of his house. I could endure whatever he threw my way over the next year and a half. Plus, I had Landon. I could hang out with him. He could pick me up. Then I didn't have to come home, because when you're riding with someone else, you're on their time. This worked out just fine for me.

"Son, I know you're hurting." My dad came over to the couch where I was sitting and placed his hand on my shoulder. "It's taken me awhile to be able to even deal with the fact of what's going on with your mom. I can't speak for her, and I don't have any answers for why this is her choice. But she's your loving mother, and we didn't tell you because—"

"You know what, Dad? Save it. There's no reason why you should have told me. As you said, she's my mother. Part of who she says she is makes up who I am."

"Exactly, and I didn't want you hearing she was gay and start questioning your own sexuality. There, okay? I said it. Your mom was ashamed, and I was scared."

Both of us just held a stare. Then we both looked away, arms crossed. There was no real wall between us, but figuratively, it was a twelve-foot brick wall that neither one of us wanted to bust through.

Then my dad just started being vulnerable. He opened up as he wept. I was surprised by what he shared.

He confessed, "I've loved your mother my entire life, but she didn't think I was enough. I just didn't satisfy her, and maybe that sent her into the arms of a woman. How do you think that made me feel? I didn't want to tell you about what was going on because I honestly didn't want you to think less of me. What kind of man can't satisfy his wife? So yes, I came, took you, and moved here. Yes, we agreed not to tell you. I don't regret keeping it from you. We temporarily spared you the pain and anguish that you're probably going through right now. I was clueless on how to help you deal with it because I've been having a hard time too."

I just reached over to my dad and held him real tight. When we were looking at each other, he could see I was broken too. I wanted to tell him none of this was his fault. I didn't know where this came from. He was right. He couldn't answer for my mom. I had so many questions, but right now I had to deal with the broken man standing in front of me. I let him know I'd be all right. Someway, somehow, we'd both be all right. This was only making us stronger, wiser, bolder, and better. Even though neither one of us could see ourselves on a better path, I was determined we would both get there. This wasn't going to ruin us.

"Look, Stone, I really do need more effort from you. It's taking you about ten minutes between each kick. Where's the hustle and get up and go? Come on, let's go. Let's do this. We've got a big game in two days," Coach Strong barked. He got in my face to pump me up during Wednesday afternoon's practice.

"Sorry, Coach, I'm just tired," I said, trying to be real with him.

"You can rest after we're done winning the state title. Right now everyone needs to be on their A game. And you might not play on offense or defense, but I still need more production out of you during practice. You know my rule. What do I say? How we practice is what?"

"How we perform," I responded with little energy.

"Exactly, so give me more. And during the game with the play clock winding down, you're not going to have all this time to set up a kick."

"I'm ready, Coach," Brick ran over and said. "He was like that yesterday. He's like that today. He's getting nervous. Just put me in."

Coach gave me a quizzical look, but he made the decision to start me. Yeah, sure I'd only played in two games, but everybody knew Brick was a bust. However, if that's who Coach wanted to go with, I really wasn't trying to fight him. And it wasn't that I didn't care about winning the game, I was all down for us getting this first playoff game behind us so we could press forward.

"Hey, Coach, let me just talk to my man right here." Landon came out of nowhere and put his arm around my neck.

Coach said, "We don't have time for lollygagging from either of you, so you talk to your boy. Work out whatever y'all need to work out. You know I'm here for you guys too. I know you guys have been through a lot, but this is our time. We all need to be focused."

"I don't feel like talking, Landon," I said.

"All right, then just hear me out," Landon started. "When I was going through all that drama a couple of weeks ago, you were there. You didn't let me wallow. You didn't let me sulk. You didn't let me forget that I was an overcomer."

"I wish it was just that easy to talk about it. Landon, seriously, I appreciate you caring, man, really. You and I been on our own rollercoaster ride with our friendship, and I'm not trying to be rude, but I don't wanna talk right now."

"So that's just supposed to make me give up? 'Cause you said you don't wanna talk right now?" Landon taunted. "We got this big ole game coming up. You know Coach is on edge. I've been watching a couple NFL games, and I never realized how tough folks were on the kicker. I'm so used to concentrating on offense and defense, but now I see people think kickers win or lose games."

"It's a team sport," I uttered, not wanting all the pressure.

"It is. We're in it together, so get your mind off whatever's bothering you."

"And if you walked into the school and saw the molester standing right there, you could just forget it and get over it?"

Landon was silent. Then he attacked. "I ain't trying to be funny, dude, but it ain't like you have anything that heavy going on anyway. I wouldn't wish that on you or anyone."

If he only knew, I thought, shaking my head. I just wanted to get to the locker room and call it a day. I wasn't a cocky football player, but I was confident. Coach Strong just needed to leave me alone and give me some time. He needed to let me practice my own way because right now I wasn't being productive. And right now, Landon was getting on my nerves.

"I haven't said this to anyone else, but I'm still shaken. If it hadn't been for folks like you getting me to open up and deal with what was going on, I know I would not have made it. I know it would have been harder. I wouldn't have been able to deal with my problems, and it just wouldn't have been good. So if you say you been through a lot, let me be there for you, man," Landon offered, popping me in the chest, desperately trying to break up some of my agony and lighten up my mood.

"All right, here it is. You wanna know? I found my mom with another woman."

"Aw snap, dude," he cried. I grabbed him by the collar and quickly held him against the outside of the building.

He threw up his hands, "I'm just saying. I'm sorry. Dang, man, I'm sorry. I know that's gotta be hard."

"You have *no* idea," I said, releasing him.

"You live with your dad, though, right? What's he saying about all this?"

"That's just it. He kept it from me for months."

"Parents just try to protect us, thinking we're still little boys. They don't even understand we got swag and stamina and are growing into men. Don't sweat them for wanting to protect you. Lots of people nowadays finally feel like they're able to come out with their ... um ... sexual orientation and be who they feel like they were meant to be."

"I get it for anybody out there in the rest of the world, but it isn't supposed to be that way for my *mom*, Landon. My dad left us three years ago. I was so angry at him, knowing it was him who probably did something wrong. She let me believe that, but really she was wrestling with her own issues. It just doesn't seem right."

"Just don't let what's going on with your mom determine who you are."

"How can it not? She's my mom. I'm a part of her. The fact that she's a lesbian is messing with my head."

"Watch it now," Landon said. "I don't know much about that other girl you dated, but I can tell when a dude is falling for a girl, and Randal is getting under your skin. If you were gay, dude, you wouldn't have it bad for a girl like that."

I knew he was right, but I wanted to work it out in my head just to be sure. Randal was making me excited. The kiss we shared was still floating in my thoughts.

"Just think on it," he said.

I went into the locker room and heard something—or someone—crashing to the floor.

"Who's there? I'm coming. Who's there?" the voice called out.

I ran to see what was going on, and it was Waxton trying to hide drugs. "Man, what are you doing? I'm sick and tired of this. I saw you the other night buying this stuff. That's it! I played your little game. People talking about they need me to be all in for Friday night's game, and you're gonna put us out, being all cracked out. We can't have our star running back strung out," I said hotly. I turned around to go and get Coach Strong.

Before I could exit, I felt something really sharp and cold against my spine. I had on shoulder pads and a jersey. Something was cutting through the T-shirt underneath.

"Don't even think about opening up your mouth to say what's going on with me. Mind your business," Wax threatened. "You got that? You understand? I tried to tell you before, white boy. You don't get a brother, and you sure don't know what can make one tick. But if you open up your mouth and get in my way, then you sure gonna find out what makes an angry black man go off."

Time was moving slowly. I kept to myself. Finally, our playoff game night was here. There was such camaraderie in the locker room. Everyone was excited. They were doing handshakes, dances, and all sorts of stuff to stay loose. I wasn't a part of any of their rituals. I tried telling myself I was okay with it, but truth be told, I was bothered by the fact that I was an outsider. I didn't know how to change it.

How could I be close with a group of guys who were clearly different from me? Especially now, when who I thought I was no longer existed. I felt like a different person. There was no way to be the same after finding out the kind of news I had weighing on my heart. And hearing that the mayor of Atlanta and other celebrities were at our playoff game only intensified my need to stay focused.

"All right, guys, it's time to gather around. The moment we've all been working so hard for is here. I know I've been tough on you this week, but the team we're playing against is fast. We can't afford any mistakes, and I needed to have you ready," Coach Strong encouraged.

"Coach, Coach, you gotta come quick! It's Wax. He's lying on the bathroom floor out cold. I can't get him to wake up, Coach. I just walked in there, and he was lying there. Something's not right." Brick was freaking out.

My heart started racing as if it was in the Indy 500. What in the world was going on? What had Waxton done? Had keeping my mouth shut been the right thing? I took a chance that he'd hurt me more than he would hurt himself. But what if he died? I just started feeling sick and nauseous, like I was about to barf.

The coaches rushed into the bathroom; several of the players followed. I couldn't breathe. Just the thought that Waxton had OD'd and I didn't do anything, didn't say anything, and didn't let anyone know he was using, sent me spiraling out of control.

"You okay?" Landon demanded, passing by me. "You're blue."

I couldn't talk. I just started hitting my chest. Landon pushed me to the nearby water fountain, put my head near the spout, and allowed the water to splash all over my face. Thankfully, that broke the tension.

"Oh my gosh. He's gotta be okay. He's gotta be okay!" I shouted.

I rushed to the bathroom, but Waxton wasn't moving. He was as still as a corpse. He had to be okay; he just had to be.

"Call the paramedics in!" Coach Strong yelled out. "Get them now! You all move out of here."

"Is he moving, Dad?" Blake yelled. "We got a game. We need him."

"He might be dead, man, and you talking about a game?" Leo barked.

"I feel a slight pulse!" Coach Grey yelled.

Shouts and heavy sighs were heard throughout the room. The trainer and Coach Grey stayed with Waxton. Coach Strong wanted the rest of us to get ready to head out.

I rushed up to him and said, "I … I gotta tell you, Coach. It's … something he's … taking. It's drugs. He's been shooting something; he's been using …"

Coach asked, "How do you know? Calm down! Tell me what you know."

"I've seen him," I admitted.

"You *what?*" Blake yelled from across the room.

"Calm down, son," Coach ordered, but Blake already got a hold of my jersey.

Blake snapped, "No, Dad. If he's known that Wax has been on drugs and didn't say nothing, then that's despicable. He could be dying!"

"I know! Don't you think I know that? I should have said something. Look in his locker for his stash."

I pushed Blake away. I needed air. I grabbed my helmet and gloves and ran out of the locker room.

The game was a blur. Way into the fourth quarter, I came out of the daze I was in. All I kept thinking about was how people around me were going through things and I just stood by, stayed quiet, and didn't get involved. I hated that I was a coward.

We were a point behind. I jogged out onto the field to score the extra point to tie it up and send the game into overtime. I only had to kick the ball through the uprights. As the long snapper hiked the ball to the holder, I started thinking about my mom and the fact that I detested her choice. What did that say about me? I hated my mom, so to punish her, I'd been avoiding her calls all week. Internally, I was struggling.

When the holder grabbed the football and turned the laces around so they wouldn't interfere with my kick, I started thinking about Waxton. I could only hope he was okay. We hadn't got any word, and it was killing me. So when I ran up to kick the ball, my game was off, and the ball missed the uprights by inches. The clock ran out, and we lost.

I felt the weight of the world on me, and not just because I was disappointed that we were out of the playoffs. I dropped to my knees in agony. I let my team down in a big way. But worse than that, I let my mom down, and I let myself down because I knew I shouldn't have just let Wax use and stay silent. I didn't know how much time passed, but I felt Coach pick me up.

"Look," he said, holding on to my collar, "we're out of it, and I'm disappointed, but I'll be doggone if I'll stand here and let you sulk. We had four turnovers tonight, son—none of which were your fault. We were in the game up until the last two plays only because of the two field goals you made earlier. When we needed to, defense couldn't stop them. When we had to, offense turned the ball over. There were so many mistakes. I am *not* going to allow you to blame yourself."

"But, Coach," I said with tears streaming down my face, "if I would have made the kick, we would have gone into overtime."

"And who's to say we would have won? I'm glad you're on my team. I'm glad we had a chance. And next year we're gonna show them, and we're going to win state. You got to stay with me, son. You got to know that we all have roles here. So whatever's going on with you, you need to get it together."

Knowing so much was stressing me, I told him the obvious. "It's Wax. It's Wax. I should have told you that—"

"No, Wax is responsible for shooting up whatever it was he took. Yeah, you should have told me, because on this team we're each other's keepers, but that's not your responsibility. We all have a part to play. We'll all be okay if we all learn to stay in our certain lane.

CHAPTER 7
Will Thrive

Just leave me alone, Coach. Let me be," I cried. I tugged away from Coach Strong's grip.

"Didn't you hear me, son? We're gonna be okay. This wasn't your fault. You can't dwell on this. We're gonna be better from this."

"Better from this? My whole team is gonna hate me."

"They got a lot of other people to hate before you. I like you, Stone. You're a man who pushes through adversity. You came in here at the start of the season and couldn't play a game for weeks. You still had to practice. You still had to adjust to these knuckleheads. I know the transition here wasn't easy, but you made sure you thrived.

You're gonna learn from this. You're gonna get better from this. You are a Lion, and Lions roar; they don't cry."

"Not making the kick lost the game for us," I mumbled.

"We all share ownership in the loss. It wasn't just you."

A sturdy parental voice spoke. "Thanks, Coach. I really appreciate you talking to my son."

I looked up when I heard my dad's voice. He was standing right there in the middle of the field with us. My dad's eyes showed sympathy.

"I got him. I know there are a lot more people who need you," my dad said to Coach Strong.

Coach shook my dad's hand. He patted me on the back and awaited a smile. Once I complied, he headed toward the press.

Showing my father how down I was, I said, "I let everybody down, Dad. Coach was just being nice, but we lost the game because of me."

"Son, even if that were true, tell me what having a pity party is going to do about it."

I remained silent. "Exactly. It won't do anything. Your head probably wasn't in the game on account of what's going on, and that's certainly not all your fault. I've been so selfish. I was only thinking of me. I was so into thinking how I wanted to protect my boy that I never realized how I was hindering you from becoming a man. You deserved to know the truth as I knew it, as soon as I had it, but I kept it away from you and that wasn't right. And I've been too prideful to come to you and apologize the way I need to."

"No, Dad, we talked."

"Yeah, we did, and I've shown you some sides of me that haven't been right. I only brought you to a black school because I wanted to you to stick out to the recruiters. And I really wanted you to have a bubble around yourself and not get too close. I didn't want them to rub off on you. I guess I was sort of a bigot. I've got some things in my past that I've got to deal with. But that shouldn't affect you."

"Wow, Dad, I can't believe you're saying this to me. I'm speechless."

"I should have said this to you a long time ago, son. You're a better man than I'll ever be, and I am proud of you that you see no color. Coach Strong is right; it's just a building block for next year. You all will go to state. I know it.

And on that big stage, you're going to make the winning kick."

I just hugged him so tight. Having his support meant the world to me. I had been tripping about wanting to be a man, but at that moment, I was just his little boy. That was more than enough.

My dad pulled away from me and said, "I think there is a beautiful lady who is waiting for a ride home. I was listening earlier when you told me you had plans. Don't ruin this. Get on with your life; enjoy your youth. Don't stay out too long, though."

My dad went over to Randal who had a precious smile on her face. I turned away because I needed to wipe away some tears. I didn't want her to see me bawling. That wasn't manly.

I heard my dad say, "I'm ER's father, Mr. Stone."

"Hello, sir. I'm Randal Raines. You have a great son."

"Yeah, I do, don't I?" my dad commented proudly.

Randal came over and grabbed my hands. "I know it was a tough game," she sympathized.

I tried turning away, but she pulled me back to her. "It's okay. I know it was a tough loss."

"I can't even believe the football season's over," I sighed.

"But y'all had a great year. And they would have lost the last two games had you not been playing. So shove that in anyone's face who wants to talk trash."

I just smiled, and we headed off the field. I was actually sort of glad I didn't rush into the locker room because now the place wasn't crowded. Everybody had gone home. It didn't take me any time to shower up, knowing that Randal was waiting.

When I came back outside, she was standing with a lady who looked familiar. I couldn't remember where I knew her from, but I knew I'd seen her before. They walked over to me.

Randal said, "This is ER."

The lady said, "Yes, ER. That's him. I'm Waxton's mother. We met in Dr. Sapp's office."

Needing her to give me updates, I said, "Yes, ma'am. Is he okay?"

"Thanks to you, the doctors say he's gonna pull through just fine."

Knowing I should have said something long ago, I replied, "Ma'am, don't thank me. I should have spoken up."

She surprised me with her response. "Get in line, boy. I should have said something too. I went through his room. I knew he was into something, but I didn't wanna make too much of a stink of it. Had you not been there and told the coaches what you knew, they wouldn't have known to check him for all those drugs. Well, he's feeling bad, which is good, but he's gonna be fine. I'm getting on back over to the hospital, but I needed to talk to Coach Strong. He told me everything. My son is a hot head, but you helped him anyway. He's gonna be okay."

The lady gave me a hug. While I felt I didn't deserve it, I sure felt better after receiving it. She patted my face. I smiled, happy that we had talked.

Randal and I drove. We parked behind a closed store. I didn't have much to say. Thinking back on all that happened, I was still overwhelmed and truly hated that I didn't make that kick.

As I gazed out the window, Randal turned my head toward hers. She started kissing me and taking off her shirt. Then she began unbuttoning my pants, but when her hand slid lower, I stopped her.

"Stop."

"No, let me make you feel great," Randal whispered.

Trying to understand why she was coming on so strong, I asked, "Is this about you needing to prove to yourself you're not gay?"

"No, I want to be with you."

"Randal, you're a virgin, right?" I asked.

With a slight attitude, she went back over to the passenger side and started fixing her clothes. "And so what? That doesn't mean that I am not ready to change that."

"Well, I am too, okay? When it's our time, it will be something. Can we make a pact to wait?"

"Sure," she agreed. I wiped away her tears when I realized she was crying.

"I care for you, and you deserve the best. I want you to be my girl. The rest will come. Kissing you tells me we want each other bad."

She gave me a little grin. She made me smile when she agreed to be my girl. I hugged her, knowing we'd be good for each other.

"Are you sure about this?" Randal nervously questioned me. We were about to walk into Lockwood High School holding hands.

"Yes. Are you?" I asked, opening the front door to the school for my new girlfriend.

"Yes," she said in the sweetest voice.

An irritating voice yelled out, "Well, isn't this a trip."

I was excited to see that Waxton was at school. However, he was truly getting under my skin. The dude needed to be appreciative. Surely someone told him I was a part of saving his hide.

"Move, Wax," I stated boldly, real tired of this same scene.

Waxton moved closer to me. "Boy, please! I stand where I want to."

"If I need to move you out of my way, I will," I cautioned.

"I heard you couldn't even kick the extra point to win the game. So how you gonna kick my tail?"

I tried to let go of Randal's hand. However, she clutched it tighter. I looked at my girl; her eyes told me to walk around him and forget the tension. I knew if I did, she and I would never have peace at this school. He was just jealous that she chose me.

"He's not worth it," she whispered.

"Talk to the fool 'cause he's trying the wrong one," Wax said to Randal. "I can't even believe you think white boy is better than me. You need a real man."

"Back up, dude!" I ordered. I jerked my hand from Randal's grasp and put my palm in Waxton's chest and pushed him over to the nearest locker. "I'm tired of playing with you."

"Fight over here!" a student screamed.

Looking in his eyes, I could tell he was high. "You're on something. Shoot, Wax, you're just out the hospital. Are you crazy?"

"No, no, you got it wrong," Wax pitifully tried to sell me. "All right, man. I'ma settle down."

"You need to get some help," I swore, letting him go. I went back over to a worried Randal.

Seeing her tense face, I assured, "Everything is okay."

"What's up with Wax?"

"It's drugs," I hesitantly whispered.

Randal sighed. It was hard. We were teens, and many of our friends were trying drugs and alcohol. Trouble was, everything that glittered wasn't gold, and some things just did not need to be tried.

Just as I turned to walk Randal to class, Waxton tackled me from behind. I was stunned. He was so spacey that it was scary. What had made this tough baller lose his swag?

Landon was nearby and rushed over to Wax. "Man, I know it's hard wrestling with the fact that Gunn molested you too."

I had the answer to my question. Waxton was taking drugs to numb his pain—a pain that was so gut-wrenching that I couldn't identify with it. But Landon could, so I hoped Wax would listen.

"You don't know nothing, man," Wax yelled, not settling down at all.

Landon said, "You can't be high at school, Wax. Besides, whatever you're taking can kill you. If ER didn't tell what he knew, you might be dead now. So ease up."

Dr. Sapp came down the hall. "Be sad to suspend folks right before the Thanksgiving break. Y'all better get to class," he drawled.

Landon and I shared a glance; we contemplated ratting Wax out. However, I could tell Landon sympathized with Wax. They had both been through something awful. Landon pushed Wax out of Dr. Sapp's view. Wax got me when he mouthed thanks my way. Guess he didn't know I cared. Landon, Randal, and I hoped Wax would be all right.

"So what's up, man? You gonna go with us to shoot some hoops or what?" Landon said into the receiver on Thanksgiving morning.

"Dude, me and you both know Blake don't want me playing no ball with y'all," I uttered, keeping things straight.

"And since when is what anyone else wants stopping you from doing what you want to do?" Landon kept on me.

"Oh, so you trying to psyche me out now?" I asked. I really appreciated that Landon was being a real friend.

"Is it working?" Landon teased.

It wasn't like my family had big plans on Thanksgiving Day, but I didn't want my dad to think that I was leaving him all alone. I really appreciated how he was there for me a few nights back when we lost the playoff game. We were going to be okay as father and son. My mother and me, well, that was a whole different story. But for now, I went to Lockwood High School, and if Landon was giving me a way to smooth things over with my tightest buddies there, then at least I had to give it a shot. All of us wanted to practice since basketball season was upon us, and we'd have to try out for the team.

About thirty minutes later, I was at the local park. As soon as I stepped on the court, Blake threw me a very hard chest pass. Why did the drama have to always start with these cats? It was like they were cheerleaders or something.

"So what's up, Blake? It's gotta be all that?" I said, knowing I had pride and was not down for dueling.

"Man, the two of y'all just need to go talk," Landon directed.

"Ain't nothing to talk about," Blake complained. "We get it."

Big, bad Leo stood there in a hostile stance. "Yeah, we get it," Leo barked, giving me a shove.

"Wait. Y'all get what?" Landon asked.

I was wondering the same thing. What was up?

"We were stupid," Blake said, smiling.

Was he pulling my leg? He held out his hand for me to slap it.

"Yeah, we were tripping," Leo revealed. "Got you!"

"And y'all ain't even mad at me about the game?" I asked, feeling they should be.

"I missed two sacks," Leo uttered.

"I threw two interceptions," Blake admitted with a shrug.

"See there," Landon said, draping his arms loosely around me and Blake. "We are all just one big, old, happy family."

"No, I'm just sick and tired of all this," Brenton suddenly yelled. Amir was trying to calm him down over in the corner. "Family *is* the problem."

"Yeah, I'm sick of all this too," Blake said, pushing past me and going over to the other two.

Obviously, there big tension brewing between the cousins. However, since I had just gotten out of my mess, I wasn't trying to get in the middle of someone else's. I stood back

"Let's just play. Six of us here. Let's do this," Landon stressed, trying to get them to focus.

I had always heard street basketball was what prepared the brothers to be able to jump, shoot, dribble, and play the heck out of some b-ball. They were brash. They were physical. They were stiff competition, but that was okay. I could handle mine. I simply had to show them that the white boy could play.

Blake, Landon, and I took on Amir, Leo, and Brenton. We killed them. Brenton looked the most bent out of shape.

Leo said, "Lots of boys trying out for basketball. Word's out, Coach is only gonna put five new players on varsity."

"We called you out here, ER, to see if we needed to be worried," Landon said, trying to catch his breath. "You've got real skills. Even with the six of us out here, one of us ain't gonna make it."

"So you guys didn't play last year?"

Landon said, "We were on JV."

"*Somebody* don't need to make it," Blake said, eluding to his cousin.

"You think you better than everybody in everything," Brenton said. "I'm sick of this. I'm out."

But Brenton didn't have a car. He looked at Amir. Amir put his thumb up.

"I'll take you home, man," Amir offered. "Catch up to y'all later."

"Let's hook up and do something later," Landon said. "We can play some games with the hotties or something."

"Yeah, let's grab all the honeys together," Blake yelled, still trying to mess with his cousin's mind.

Blake shot Landon a look. That Charli girl was going to need to choose between the two cousins. If not, one of them would kill the other.

I hadn't seen Randal in a couple of days. I wasn't trying to avoid her, but we were out for Thanksgiving, and she knew I needed my privacy to figure so much out. I loved that she wasn't sweating me, but it was a holiday. I wanted to see my girl.

Everyone wanted to hang out. Landon told me that Eva told him that some of the other cheerleaders had been a little rough on Randal. So I called her house and her mom answered.

"Hi, ma'am, this is ER. I'm Randal's friend."

"Yes, ER, how you doing?" Mrs. Raines said in a nice voice.

"I'm good. I was just hoping that I could see Randal a little later on. Some of us were just trying to hang out and play cards and games and stuff and—"

"Oh, we'd love to have you guys come over. She's been sulking a little bit. She's getting ready now for Thanksgiving dinner, but you guys come on over this evening. I won't say a word. She'll be so surprised."

"You sure?"

"Yeah, trust me. It'll make her day."

After dinner we all met up over at Randal's house. We didn't go to the door until everyone got there. There were already a lot of cars there, and I was a little hesitant about going in.

Eva said, "Please. She's going to be so shocked. She likes you, you know."

"I like her too," I admitted.

When Randal saw us, her jaw dropped. She gave me such a big hug, and I was thrilled that we could spend some time together with our friends. Brenton didn't show up, so it was five guys with five girls.

Randal's dad was cool and so was her brother, who was home from college, but they both let us know they were watching. After a couple hours of fun and good food, it was time to head home.

I had worked some things out with my friends. I had worked some things out with my father. I was working through some stuff with football, and I just needed to be happy with that.

When I pulled into my driveway and saw my mom's car, I froze. We hadn't talked in over a week. She called me, but I needed tons of space. Manning up, I went to the door.

My father asked, "You cool?" when he saw me walk into the room.

My mom stood to her feet. "Hi, ER, I hope it's okay I'm here."

Studying them both for a second, I said, "Yes, I'm cool with it. It's fine."

"I'll let y'all talk," my dad said, and he left.

She came over to me and admitted, "I know you haven't returned my calls for a reason, but it's Thanksgiving. What I am most grateful for is you, sweetheart. You've grown up so much. You're almost a man. I at least owed you the decency to tell you what was going on with me. I should have trusted you. I certainly didn't intend for you to find out that way. I didn't come here to ask for your forgiveness about my choices. But I need to ask you to forgive me for not trusting you. I blocked you out, but when you love someone, you've got to trust them with tough information."

"When did you decide you're gay, Mom?" I asked, cutting to what I wanted to know. "And why?"

"I don't know, son. I wrestled with it for years. Connecting with a woman is just something that I can't explain. It just is. I don't want you to hate me because of it."

"I know being gay isn't contagious. But did I do something wrong to make you like this?" I said, becoming vulnerable.

"Son, no! My choices have nothing to do with you."

"Well, why didn't dad want me living there?"

"He said he shared with you some of his reasons, but honestly, I was scared ... Scared that if you found out, you would never want to speak to me again, and I couldn't bear it. I took the coward's way out. I let him take my son, but now I can't eat, sleep, or breathe. The only thing I can do is think about you and hope that I haven't ruined our relationship for good. I can't be happy if you're not in my life."

Tears poured down her face. I stepped to her and instinctively held her tight. There was a lot I didn't understand, but she made the first step toward me. She was helping me try and rationalize it all. She was treating me with the trust our relationship had lacked. She was baring her soul. For so long, I felt like I meant nothing in her world, but she cleared all that up. I was grateful.

The move to Lockwood High had been one that changed so much for me, but it brought out the truth. It also showed me what pride was all about. Basically, I learned that I couldn't control other people's choices. All teams have issues, no matter the color of the players' skin, but the things you go through don't have to hold you down. If you embrace the bad, learn from it, and strive to stand for what's right, you will thrive.

STEPHANIE PERRY MOORE is the author of many YA inspirational fiction titles, including the *Payton Skky* series, the *Laurel Shadrach* series, the *Perry Skky Jr.* series, the *Yasmin Peace* series, the *Faith Thomas Novelzine* series, the *Carmen Browne* series, the *Morgan Love* series, and the *Beta Gamma Pi* series. Mrs. Moore speaks with young people across the country, encouraging them to achieve every attainable dream. She currently lives in the greater Atlanta area with her husband, Derrick, and their three children. Visit her website at www.stephanieperrymoore.com.

DERRICK MOORE is a former NFL running back and currently the developmental coach for the Georgia Institute of Technology. He is also the author of *The Great Adventure* and *It's Possible: Turning Your Dreams into Reality*. Mr. Moore is a motivational speaker and shares with audiences everywhere how to climb the mountain in their lives and not stop until they have reached the top. He and his wife, Stephanie, have co-authored the *Alec London* series. Visit his website at www.derrickmoorespeaking.com.

WANT A DIFFERENT

point of view?

JUST *flip* THE BOOK!

WANT A DIFFERENT
point of view?

JUST *flip* THE BOOK!

STEPHANIE PERRY MOORE is the author of many YA inspirational fiction titles, including the *Payton Skky* series, the *Laurel Shadrach* series, the *Perry Skky Jr.* series, the *Yasmin Peace* series, the *Faith Thomas Novelzine* series, the *Carmen Browne* series, the *Morgan Love* series, and the *Beta Gamma Pi* series. Mrs. Moore speaks with young people across the country, encouraging them to achieve every attainable dream. She currently lives in the greater Atlanta area with her husband, Derrick, and their three children. Visit her website at www.stephanieperrymoore.com.

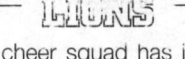

The Lockwood High cheer squad has it *all*—sass, looks, and all the right moves. But everything isn't always as perfect as it seems. Because where there's cheer, there's drama. And then there are the ballers—hot, tough, and on point. But what's going to win out—life's pressures or their NFL dreams?

CHEERANDAL
Drama

Randal Raines might be the shyest girl on the squad, but the guys think she is fly ...

SOUTHWARK LIBRARIES

SK 2046857 1

SHAKE IT

Stephanie Perry Moore

SADDLEBACK
EDUCATIONAL PUBLISHING

CHEER DRAMA

Always Upbeat

Keep Jumping

Yell Out

Settle Down

Shake It

SADDLEBACK
EDUCATIONAL PUBLISHING
www.sdlback.com

Copyright © 2012 by Saddleback Educational Publishing
All rights reserved. No part of this book may be reproduced in any form or
by any means, electronic or mechanical, including photocopying, recording,
scanning, or by any information storage and retrieval system, without the written
permission of the publisher. SADDLEBACK EDUCATIONAL PUBLISHING
and any associated logos are trademarks and/or registered trademarks of
Saddleback Educational Publishing.

ISBN-13: 978-1-61651-888-2
ISBN-10: 1-61651-888-X
eBook: 978-1-61247-622-3

Printed in Guangzhou, China
0812/CA21201149

16 15 14 13 12   1 2 3 4 5

To Vanessa Davis Griggs and Victoria Christopher Murray

You both are writing angels. I thank you both for helping me in my writing career. It is only for your help and love that I have had some closed doors opened to me. Many days I didn't know how I'd make it as a writer, but you were there to help me find my way. You told me to shake off the negative thoughts and shake on a positive mentality. May every reader dare to find themselves and reach their full potential.

Keep working your pen … I love you!

ACKNOWLEDGEMENTS

You are young, so it is natural to wonder who you are. Where are you going? What do you want in life? Who are your real friends? Will you ever have someone to love you? And many, many other questions, but if no questions are asked, there will be no answers.

However, too many questions can overwhelm you. Feeling like you know nothing can be depressing. Take life one day at a time. Set goals and work toward them. If you don't like something about yourself, don't wallow. Change it for the better. Sometimes seeking answers can lead you down paths you don't want to tread. Point: though you might not fully know who you are, you are someone special. So handle yourself with care. Shake it, don't break it!

Here is a considerable thank you to everyone who helps move my writing to the next level.

Acknowledgements

For my parents, Dr. Franklin and Shirley Perry Sr., thank you for allowing me to shake it while young. Your guidance helped me dream big.

For my publisher, especially the office staff at Saddleback, thank you for letting me shake it with you by being a part of your mission. Your belief helps me live a purpose-filled life.

For my extended family: brother, Dennis Perry, mother-in-law, Ann Redding, brother-in-Christ, Jay Spencer, godmother, Marjorie Kimbrough, and goddaughter, Danielle Lynn, thank you for helping me shake it daily as you help me keep my head up high. Your support makes me feel good.

For my assistants: Joy Spencer, Keisha King, and Shaneen Clay, thank you for assisting me in shaking out my thoughts. Your diligence helps me keep the novel real and right for readers.

For my friends whom I love to pieces: Leslie Perry, Lakeba Williams, Nicole Smith, Torian Colon, Loni Perriman, Kim Forest, Vickie Davis, Kim Monroe, Jamell Meeks, Michele Jenkins, Lois Barney, Perlicia Floyd, Veronica Evans, Laurie Weaver, Taiwanna Brown-Bolds, Matosha Glover, Yolanda Rodgers-Howsie, Dayna Fleming, Denise Gilmore, and Deborah Bradley, thank you for getting me

to shake it and truly live life. Your friendship helps me be the best I can be.

For my teens: Dustyn, Sydni, and Sheldyn, thank you for being the inspiration that makes me shake it twenty-four-seven. Your existence helps me long to protect and provide for you.

For my husband, Derrick, thank you for shaking it with me. Your partnership helps me feel complete.

For my new readers, thank you for finding this novel and shaking off anything that holds you back from reading it. Your future helps me stay inspired to write on.

And my Lord, thank you for blessing me with a writing talent to shake. Your Grace for me helps me not look back to what I used to be, but press on to what you'll have me to be.

CHAPTER 1

Move Closer

I was truly happy for my girlfriend Eva Blount when she walked out on the field as the eleventh-grade homecoming attendant. Eva was the exact opposite of me. She was boisterous and bold. I was subdued and shy.

I always thought of Eva as a remarkable young woman. She really deserved the honor to offset all that she had just gone through. She was raped and her assaulter made a video that was seen by everyone we knew.

Our football team was winning for the ninth time in a row. As a cheerleader, I should have been psyched, pumped, or thrilled. However, I went through the motions and was a bit melancholy. I

had not gone through anything severe like Eva. I had not caught my dad cheating on my mom like Charli. I did not get shot like Ella. My mother did not need to go into rehab like Hallie's. Yeah, my girls had serious issues, but they all seemed very giddy.

All my girls had a man to escort them to the homecoming dance. Though Charli had been dumped by our starting quarterback, Blake Strong, she had a new boyfriend, his cousin Brenton. Everyone knew Blake wanted her back, and she was even entertaining it. But Charli's date to homecoming was Brenton. Hallie had Amir Knight, a guy who'd watched her from afar and wanted her desperately. So Hallie had a date. Ella fell for Leo Steele and made it her personal mission to help him when he was homeless. While I still think he is having a hard time, his days are brighter because he knows he has a girlfriend who cares. So there was Ella's date. Even Eva, who never wanted to settle down, in my opinion, had found her soul mate, Landon King. Landon was our star wide receiver, who had a similar scandal rock his world. The news hit around the same time as Eva's. Landon had

been molested as a kid, and the man who did it returned to wreak more havoc. Thankfully, Landon faced his demons, and the molester was probably going to spend decades in prison. Yeah, Eva and Landon were both survivors. As their friendship grew, he asked her out to the homecoming dance a few days ago.

Everyone had someone but me. While that in and of itself made me feel horrible, watching the four of them talk about what was to come made me realize how different I was from them. I felt that way at my old school. I was biracial. My mother was white. My dad was black. At my old school, the majority of kids were white, and I didn't think I fit in. I always heard if you had a drop of chocolate in you, you were considered black. When my dad gave me the opportunity to come to this new school, which was the opposite, my mom was not for it but she reluctantly agreed.

For the last few years, the five of us girls have been inseparable. However, my girls were always the ones doing the talking. Words didn't come to me naturally, but it was probably because I just did not have my own voice yet. I had been in school with mostly white folks all my

life. While I didn't fit in there, here I did not feel black either. I did not feel as authentic as them. I know it was crazy, but it was how I felt.

I am sure if you talked to different mixed people, they could all give you different explanations about who they thought they were. Some would say they were white. Some would say they were black. Some would say they truly were mixed. Some would say they were neither. Some would be offended you asked. Some would avoid the question. Those like me wished they had an answer.

I wanted to be excited for my friends. That was who I was. I was never a jealous person. I did envy the fact that they were confident in their own skin. I felt like my body was not really mine. If I looked in the mirror, I felt like I did not know where I belonged. I was a junior in high school for goodness' sake. It was time for me to step up, be happy, and get excited about my future. The problem was that I never really had a past to hold on to. The holidays were coming up, and my parents were arguing where we were going to spend them. Even though we were in the twenty-first century, it seemed ludicrous

to me that my grandparents were still not fine with their union. Who shared the brunt of my folks' anguish? Their offspring—me.

I was actually surprised when Eva came over to me and said, "Look, I don't have to go to this dance. Landon just asked me at the last minute, but you and I can hang out. You know this getting dressed-up stuff ... I could really leave it."

"No, you deserve to be Cinderella. Out of the wicked stuff that has happened to you, I would never take this moment away. Mr. King is real excited. He gave you the ball after making a touchdown tonight, didn't he? Come on, Eva, Landon likes you. It's so obvious."

"Please, Landon King is just like his boy, Leo Steele, always trying to have all the women. He can't settle down."

"Ella tamed Leo."

"Well, I'm nobody's ringmaster and this isn't the circus. He's definitely not going to make a fool out of me. I'm sure I'm going to get certain looks just because he's taking me to the dance. You know how the chicks in this school are about these ballers."

"Yeah, particularly since they've been winning," I said, agreeing to the drama we'd been through this year with girls. "But seriously, I love you for caring. I just got a lot of stuff on my mind. My parents are here, and I'm going to go with them. You guys have a good time."

"I thought you were going to come with us," Hallie said loudly when she heard I was jetting. "You were going to help us get dressed. Just because you're not going doesn't mean—"

"Shhh!" Eva said to her. "She doesn't want the whole world knowing her business."

The four of them were happy, and I did not want them at it over me. I quickly gave them all hugs.

I said, "Calm down. Y'all have fun. And I don't want to hear about no cheer drama."

I went from one arguing group to another. As I got in the car, I heard my parents going at it. I was baffled, so I listened in to make out their beef.

"I just don't understand why you wanted her to come to this school," my mom whined. "These kids are running around here like animals. People fighting. Gang kids talking about

shooting. Shucks, I had to watch my purse because this one boy looked like he was going to grab it," she vented.

"And where is all of this coming from, Dana?" my dad asked. "You're acting like you have issues with black people now. It's just a high school game, homecoming at that. A lot of alumni came back, the band was hyped, and fans were drinking, so they got a little loud. We can't let our children have a problem with black people."

"I know," my mom agreed. "I'm sensitive. My daughter is one. My son in college is one, and my husband is one."

Hot, I cut in and said, "So I'm not white?"

"Yes, you're white, honey, but you're black too. See, Kenny, look at what you're doing. You're getting her all upset."

"She ain't upset with me," my dad shouted.

Not needing anyone to speak for me, I said, "I'm not upset at anyone, Mom. I'm just asking. Are you saying I'm not white even in your eyes?"

"Where is this coming from, Randal?" my dad asked in an upset tone.

"Never mind, Dad," I said quickly, shutting down.

My dad softened. "Pumpkin, did someone ask you something like that today? You have a problem being black?"

"So you don't think I'm white either," I said, shaking.

"You're not answering the question."

"Neither are you," I said back to him, actually surprised I had gumption.

My parents grumbled at my response. They started talking to one another. I was in a daze.

When one of them called my name, I said, "I'm sorry, guys, I just have a headache. Let's just not talk on the way home."

They obliged my request. I saw my parents looking at each other, worried that their daughter was going through a serious identity crisis. No one wanted to tell me what they thought I really was. Maybe I needed to go deeper and find out what I wanted to be. Did I need to let others define me? I surely was not lying. I just wanted to be normal, but I felt so far from that.

"Oh my goodness, last night was the best night of my life," Ella said with sheer excitement. Anyone could see her joy.

"I know, and you looked so pretty. The guys were handsome. The night felt like a fairytale," Charli chimed in.

"I know, right?" laid-back Eva added. "I didn't think I would enjoy myself, but it was actually kind of fun. Landon and I showed you guys up on the dance floor. He's cool."

"Yeah, and you like him," Hallie said as she teased Eva. "And that dress you wore, girl. Who knew you could go so traditional?"

It was actually good to know Eva learned something since her horrific ordeal. Now she probably would never go out in public with her assets showing the way they used to. She was calling us boring because we covered up so much. Now she was getting compliments for doing the same. It was fun to witness.

However, that was the only part of this that was fun. Again, I did not wish ill on any of my four best friends, but I did not feel included either. They were talking all around my head. We only had a few minutes for break. We were at cheerleading practice, and we were supposed to be getting ready for regionals. Not once did they stop and ask, "Randal, what did you do? Randal,

we missed you there. We have pictures. Do you want to see?" Nope, they just kept talking and forgot all about me.

"What great friends you all are," I finally yelled when I'd had it up to my hair.

"What's wrong with you?" Ella asked. She came over and tried to put her arm around my shoulder.

I jerked away. Her sympathy was not what I wanted or needed. They all looked at me pitifully. That action angered me further.

"Randal, we didn't mean to hurt your feelings," Hallie replied, seeing me seething.

"I don't want you guys to look at me like you pity me. And don't even try to stop me from going back to practice. I've stuck by each and every one of you, and now that you all have your lives figured out, you forget about me. You don't even think about how this affects me. You're just so selfish, and that hurts worst of all. I've spent three years building one-sided friendships."

Eva boldly voiced, "Randal, why are you sitting over there lying and whining?"

"*Lying?* Excuse me, Eva?"

Eva continued, "You never say more than two words to people. What do you mean stick by folks? When we need you to say something, you won't say anything. And now, obviously, you wanted to go to the dance, but you told us all emphatically that you *didn't* want to attend. Now that we've come back after having a good time—"

Cutting her off, I said, "No, don't hesitate. Say what you mean. You guys had a blast, and it's not your fault that no one wanted to take me out. I might not say anything, Eva, but be clear I'm always there in spirit. I always care about what's going on with you guys, so much so that sometimes I can't sleep at night because of how some of your problems affect me."

I just walked out of their presence and went to stand in line to start practice. I could not hold back the tears that wanted to flow. I was really down on everything. I could not explain it.

"Uh, Randal, I'd like to see you in my office please," Coach Woods, our cheer coach, called out to me.

"Yeah, Coach," I said with little emotion.

"Okay, Miss Raines, what's going on with you today? You PMSing on me?"

Anytime someone gained a little weight, Coach thought it was PMS. Anytime someone didn't feel right, she thought it was PMS. Somebody came in with an attitude, she thought it was PMS. Honestly, I wished that was the case, because it would mean in a couple of days my mood would have swept back to the positive side. Truth be told, I had been in a slump for a while. This whole semester I had not said much of anything. Watching everyone else go through so much drama drained me. I didn't say a word.

"Well, if there's nothing we need to talk about, I need you to deal with it. In order for us to qualify for state, we have to do well at regionals. All of us need to be on the same page, and you of all people know this. You've never given me a problem on the squad. No attitude, no lip, no sass, and your performances have been stellar. Right when we go to crunch time, I need you to stay on your A game."

I usually rode home with Charli or Hallie, but today I was not in the mood, so I texted my mom and asked her to pick me up.

"Hey, sweetie," she said when I got to her car. It was as if we'd had no drama the night before.

"Is everything okay with your friends? You didn't want to ride with the girls? Did you need to talk to me about anything?"

My mom was acting like I was suicidal or something. I'm glad that she could sense I was struggling. However, the way she was trying to relate to me was a lot more annoying than it was helpful.

My mother was a caterer. I looked in the back of her car. It was filled with leftover goodies, pots, pans, and other objects she used to decorate her presentation table with.

"Oh, Mom, I hope I didn't get you to leave your catering job early."

"No, no, no, I was already headed home. You called me at the right time."

Making small talk, I said, "Was it a good day?"

I wanted to be close to my mom, I did. We just never connected. She wanted me to be the pageant-type girl that she had been. She had no idea what to do with my curly hair. Long ago, I caught her on the phone with her girlfriend, crying. She was telling her she wished my hair was straight. From that day on, I did too. I was

five back then. Now I was seventeen, and I was feeling some of the same emotions.

"I was with Mrs. Collins. Becca asked about you," my mom offered.

Becca was my best friend back in middle school. I had not seen her since then. We hadn't spoken since I moved to the other side of Atlanta. I left a great school in East Cobb to come to another great school in Metro Atlanta. The culture of both schools determined who I was, and since I was now hanging with the African American kids, I really had not reached out to my old friends. All of them were white.

"She misses you. She just found you on Facebook and friended you. You should talk to her. Call her, darling. There's nothing wrong with new friends, but you can't forget the old ones. You remember the motto from Girl Scouts: One is silver and one is gold."

"I don't know if that was a motto, Mom. It's just a song we used to sing."

"Well, whatever it is, it's a sweet thought," my mom said.

The words of the song did make a lot of sense. Becca always did understand me. Though

that was middle school, maybe our connection would still be as strong.

When I got home, I immediately looked on my Facebook page. As my mom said, there was her friend request, Becca Collins. I accepted it.

"Well, about darn time," she immediately messaged me back. "I reached out to you a month ago and reached out to you two weeks ago. It takes your mom to come to my house for you to care about your old friend? What's going on, girl? This picture you posted looks beautiful. We have to connect."

Honestly, I wanted to pick up the phone and call her. That's how much I longed to be close to someone. Not to be too pushy, I rethought that plan. I just messaged her back.

I said, "Yeah, you're right. I got to get better at keeping in touch."

Then she messaged me back and said, "What are you doing tonight? Our school has a game. Your mom is supposed to be going to the movies with my mom and some friends. Maybe she can drop you off at Grovehill's stadium."

I took a second to respond. "Maybe you'll see me."

"I miss you, Randal."

Just seeing those words on the screen made me smile. I had not had anything to smile about for a long time. I got up, went and found my mom, and told her of my desire to hang out at the Giants' game. With plans made, I went back to my room, fell on my bed, clasped my hands together, and screamed. I finally had a life outside of my girls. Maybe I could find my way after all, and though I still did not have the answers, I could move one step in the right direction.

"So we'll be there to swoop you up in just a minute," Charli said into the receiver.

She spoke just as demanding as she always was. The bossy girl assumed I had no plans, like I was just sitting there waiting and ready to be picked up whenever she made time for me.

"No need to come. I've already got plans."

"Huh? She's got plans," Charli said to someone else.

Hallie took the phone. "Okay, so what plans do you have? We tolerated your little temper tantrum at practice today, but you know we love you, so don't trip. What do you want us to say?

We're sorry or whatever. There's a big game in DeKalb County. Stephenson is playing MLK; we got to be there."

"We don't have to be nowhere. You guys are on your way out the door, and you're going to call me last minute?" I sassed. "Thanks but no thanks; I have plans."

Hallie just huffed and gave Charli back the phone. "Randal, will you talk to me? I know you were right earlier. You have been there for all of us. It must be tough that we went to the home-coming dance with guys, and you didn't. That's because most guys here are jerks and can't see. You're the cutest of us all, girl, with your mixed behind."

"Wait, what is that supposed to mean? Why can't it just be me? Why does it have to be be-cause I'm mixed that I'm cute?"

"Okay, why are you so sensitive about this? Everybody knows when you put a little cream with the chocolate it comes out fly and sweet. No issues."

"You know what? I'm not in the mood to hang out with you guys. Like I said, I have plans."

"Where are you going?"

"None of your business."

"Oh, so it's like that? Do you have a guy we don't know about?"

"Why does it have to be a guy? Why does everything about you girls have to revolve around guys? Just because you got two fawning over you—and that makes your day—doesn't mean everyone else should put such hot stock in it, okay?"

"I don't know what you're talking about, Randal. Brenton is my boyfriend, and I'm not flirting with Blake or trying to make something happen there," Charli defended, knowing I'd hit a nerve.

"If you want to tell yourself that, fine. But if we're truly friends like you claim, then you wouldn't sell me a log hidden in the box as if it was a brand new TV."

"What are you talking about, Randal?"

"Forget it," I said, remembering when my dad thought he'd gotten a good deal and came running in the house telling my mom he bought us a new flat screen TV. It was hot off of the truck, and the guy would not let him open it because he had to keep moving when he dropped it off. My mom told my dad that he should leave

hustles alone. My dad agreed when he opened up the box and saw a log carefully placed inside instead of the TV he paid for.

Basically, I did not want Miss Spoiled-Brat-Hot-to-Trot Charli Black to sell me a bill of goods. She loved having two guys fight over her, and while I didn't hear everything that had gone on at the dance, it was all over Facebook. When Brenton went to get some punch, Blake took Charli on the dance floor for a slow number. When he saw Brenton looking, he kissed Charli, and she did not pull away. She ended up explaining to Brenton that she was caught off guard, but I knew her. She had been dating Blake since ninth grade. I was told Brenton liked her since middle school. Both cousins were hot, and they were both crazy about her.

"Well, just think what you want and do what you want. Just don't say we didn't try to hang out with you."

"Like you're doing me the biggest favor in the world? I'm an afterthought. You know what? Tonight, don't think about me at all." I hung up the phone.

"Randal, you ready, dear?" my mom asked right on cue.

"Yes, ma'am." I quickly grabbed my purse and rushed to the car.

"See, I'm so glad I told you to reconnect with Becca. How happy are you that you are going to reconnect?"

"You miss her mom and your other friends, huh?"

"I do."

"Do you even like your life?" I asked curiously.

She looked at me and gave me some pooh-pooh answer. She did not go deep. She did not really let me in. She made her choice, and it cost her a lot. She did not want me to know any of that and did not realize I already knew she regretted some of her sacrifices. She and I could never be close. She wasn't real.

"So how do you plan on connecting with Becca?" she asked.

"I have her cell number."

"You guys have talked?"

"No, she gave it to me on Facebook, and she told me to call her if I came."

"Wait, she doesn't know you're coming?"

"I think I told her. I don't know. I'm not sure. I'll be okay," I grumbled.

"Are you sure? What if you don't have any-one to hang out with?"

"Mom, go to the movies and enjoy your friends. I'll see you after, okay?"

"You're my baby, and I just want you to be okay," she said, placing her hand on my hand before I exited.

When I walked toward the stadium, I really appreciated that gesture. Even though I was not her peer, and even though I knew she had her own struggles because of her choice of a black guy, she loved us. She wanted me to be happy, and she was extremely protective. I was her daughter, and while she might have wanted me to look like her, I knew she would not trade me for anything in the world.

Grovehill was a beautiful new school. I could see why my mom was upset when my dad moved us. It was the opposite of Lockwood. No band was jamming, no dance team was throwing down, and the parking lot was full of tailgaters. At Lockwood, you better bring some money to get something at the concession stand or put a little hustle in your purse to snack on. This place was so pristine. Blondes, brunettes, and

redheads were everywhere. There were some black folks present too, but they were certainly in the minority at this school event.

Seeing people with their friends, I decided to call Becca. But there was a part of me who liked being a fly on the wall at this game. No one knew who I was, and I could just watch and admire their lives, wishing I fit in like that. Knowing that I did want some type of social life, and to get out of my funk, I texted Becca.

"I am here."

Quickly, she responded, "Who is this?"

Confirming I was nobody, I typed, "Randal."

"Oh, I'm standing with some friends by the concession stand. Where are you?"

"I'm by the concession stand."

I looked around the concession stand, trying to find Becca. She did not have a recent picture of herself on Facebook. She had a baby picture up. I was looking at some Goth girls who looked like they could have starred in *The Girl with the Dragon Tattoo*. When one of them stepped to me real close, I stepped back.

"What, you don't remember me?" Becca laughed. She put her arms out to hug me tight.

"Becca?" I wondered.

She almost looked like a boy. One side of her head was shaved. She had piercings in her nose, chin, and neck. She looked scary.

As she squeezed me, she said, "You are so beautiful."

I was extremely uncomfortable. She looked at me like I was dessert. Actually, I was shaking on the inside, knowing at that moment that I did not want to move closer.

Reduce Stress

I pulled back from Becca's embrace. She looked at me as if I should have liked it. I frowned, assuring her I did not. Three girls were with her, and two of them were hugged up with each other in a very strange way. Of those two, one looked like a girl. She had on tight jeans and was dressed real cute. The other one, who I first mistook as a boy, had her hands deep in the cute dresser's back pocket and was squeezing her behind.

"Aren't you gonna introduce me to your friend?" the last of the three girls asked Becca.

"Randal, this is Savannah," Becca said. Savannah looked at me and then gave Becca a passionate kiss.

My mouth hung open so wide that my entire fist could fit into it. Somewhere between eighth and eleventh grade, Becca had come out of the closet. She wasn't sort of gay. She wasn't maybe gay. She was all the way gay, and I was uncomfortable. She misunderstood my awe.

When she saw my reaction, Becca stepped to me and said, "No worries, she's not my girlfriend. I still got room to love you."

Was she out of her mind? Or did she think I was out of mine? No way was I a lesbian. Becca and Savannah moved away and kept kissing.

"So that's really odd, isn't it?" I heard a male voice behind me say.

I turned to see a guy from my school. It was the white kicker. ER was so handsome and cool.

"Are you all right?"

"Barely, seeing that," I uttered, really unsure if I was okay or not.

"What are you doing all the way over here? I didn't know this was your scene," ER said.

"I would have gone to this high school, but I left right after middle school," I responded, wondering about him as well. "Is this where you came from?"

"Yup, I was a Giant," he said, referring to Grovehill's mascot.

Becca saw a guy standing near me, and she quickly came to me. "Come on, we're going to go sit in the stands."

"You can hang out with me if you want," ER offered. He perceived that I was completely uncomfortable with the thought of hanging with Becca and her crew.

"I'll catch you later," I said to Becca.

Becca gave ER an annoyed look, like she didn't want me to hang out with him. I didn't know what all of that was about. However, having to choose between a guy I didn't know well but seemed upstanding, and a girl I thought I knew but appeared scary, I chose hanging out with the guy.

"Thank you," I said. We walked over to the Giants' side to take our seats near the band. "I would have been so uncomfortable."

"How do you know Becca?" he asked.

"Huh? I can't hear you," I said.

"How do you know Becca?" he repeated.

"She was my best friend."

"Oh, so are you—"

"What? Gay?" I paused, assessing ER's face. "No, I'm not"

"Yeah, you seemed a little caught off guard by their PDA."

"I hadn't connected with her in ages, and I'm just shocked."

"Well, she's been like that ever since I've known her."

"How do you like Lockwood? It's, like, really different from this," I said.

I was really curious if he liked our school. I sort of fit in because I did have some black in my blood. But this dude was white as snow. Though he still had swag, he was a fish out of water at Lockwood.

"I've adjusted," he commented. "People are people. Color doesn't bother me. It's culture that gets me sometimes."

Clearly, I knew what he meant. Black folks had a tendency to be loud, and there was never a dull moment at Lockwood. White kids weren't necessarily as boisterous, but they still had their ways of making a fuss. Neither school, no matter how fancy or cool, was perfect, and teenagers were all pretty much the same.

ER continued, "I just try to make the most of wherever I am. I know I wanna be out there on that football field."

Word was out that he was supposedly a great kicker. I knew a lot of the players were mad that he wasn't able to play yet. Something about not being eligible through the Georgia High School Sports Association. I did not know the whole story, and we didn't have any classes together. I had seen girls checking him out. The few white girls we had at Lockwood, of course, but the sistas were checking him out too. It usually was that way with someone new, but the flavor died out after a couple of weeks. He'd been there pretty much all semester, and no one had a lock on him.

"How did you know who I was?" I asked, still thankful that he had rescued me from the awkward situation.

"I wasn't sure if you were from my school. I just took a chance. When I got a little closer and saw your face, I knew you were the cheerleader who hung with Leo and Amir's girls."

Venting, I complained, "Yeah, but now that they got boyfriends, our closeness has changed."

"Yeah, people get connected and lose their mind. Especially girls sometimes." He shrugged. "Why aren't you connected to anybody?" he asked.

I just shrugged my shoulders. "Me? What about you? There are lots of girls who want you."

"Want him how?" an obnoxious girl butted into our conversation.

I turned and couldn't believe it was Jillian Grayson.

"Randal?" she questioned

"Jillian?" I scoffed.

There was no love lost between us. We hated each other in middle school. She always thought I was a mulatto mess and not good enough to be in her clique. If it wasn't for Becca always including me, middle school would have been torture.

"ER, why are you talking to her?" Jillian snapped. Then the chick growled my way, "And I know *you're* not trying to take my boyfriend."

ER rolled his eyes. Now the cat was out of the bag. Jillian was his girlfriend. No further explanation was needed as to why he wasn't into any Lockwood girls. She had on the latest fashions and looked beautiful. Though she was spoiled and obnoxious, she was classy dresser.

Yep, I had my answer as to why. ER had not been trying to get to know any girls. He already had one, and she was a handful.

"We were just talking," I said, releasing the cat from my tongue.

ER huffed and said, "Jill, chill."

"Well, I barely get to see you anymore since you moved to *that* school," Jillian whined, as if ER went to a school with animals or something.

"What's wrong with *that* school? That's the one *I* go to, Jillian," I stated boldly.

Dripping with sarcasm, she responded, "Go figure." She turned to her beau and used a nicer tone. "ER, c'mon, babe, everyone wants to see you. You two can talk at lunchtime at Backwoods High."

"It's called Lockwood High." I rolled my eyes.

"Whatevs."

To ease the tension I said, "It was good talking to you, ER. I'll see you later.

I stood up on the bleachers and walked away. I had no idea where I was walking. I didn't wanna be around all that. Ironically, when I looked back, he was looking at me. I quickly turned away. It was an interesting feeling I'd never felt

before. With his choice of girlfriends, I needed to forget the feeling before it had a chance to grow.

"Hey, Mom, the game's not over yet, but I can come on out if you're here," I said in response to my mom's incoming call.

"No, sweetie, I'm on my way home."

"Huh? Well, how am I supposed to get home?"

"Well, Becca wants more time with you. Her mom talked to her when we were done, and since the game wasn't over, we just decided y'all can catch up all night. I couldn't rush you on back. You always say I cut off the party too soon."

"Wait, wait, Mom, what are you saying?" I said, trying to figure this all out.

"You're gonna go home with Becca and spend the night with her. I'll pick you up early tomorrow."

"Um, Mom, no that won't work," I pleaded. Becca was walking my way, and I shook harder than an earthquake at the thought of having to spend time with her.

"Hey, there you are," Becca said. She snatched the phone. "I got her, Mom, so don't worry."

Though she used to call my mom, *Mom*, we weren't cool like that anymore. I tried to grab my phone back, but before I could explain to my mom that this was a bad idea, Becca disconnected the call.

"What are you doing?" I shouted.

"There's no need to make your mom worry, so just relax."

I couldn't even enjoy the end of the game. Grovehill was winning, but these folks at my old school were nuts. Deep down, I wondered why in the world I didn't take Charli up on her offer to hang out with them. At least I knew what I was getting into with them. And while I might not have a voice around those girls, at least I wasn't being forced to witness a lifestyle that was foreign to me. Savannah and Becca were grossing me out with their outward affection. Since I knew they supposedly were not exclusively dating each other, I hated to see what it would look like if they were monogamous. Nobody seemed to be disturbed by their actions but me.

When the game was over, Savannah said, "I want to spend the night too. You're not gonna get to have fun with Randal without me."

"I didn't invite you," Becca said to her.

I looked at the two of them like, *There ain't gonna be no fun!* What did Savannah think would happen? This was crazy. When we got in the car, Becca's mom was so happy to see me.

I complained, "I got a headache. If you don't mind, would it be too much of an inconvenience to take me home."

"Well, your mom said you could stay, honey. And that is a little far. I've got aspirin in the house. Don't worry about it. I will make up your bed right away."

In my mind, I was thinking bed was the absolute last place I wanted to be. Didn't this lady know her daughter was into girls? That whole scene frightened me.

"I don't have any clothes," I uttered, trying to come up with an excuse.

Mrs. Collins said, "No worries. Becca's got plenty of things you could put on. You girls are still the same size."

Did Becca even like being called a girl? I wasn't trying to be funny, but this was weird. I hoped that I wasn't being judgmental, but I just didn't want to be a part of her world.

When we got to her house, her mom immediately handed me the aspirin. I didn't take it right away.

Becca said, "All right, Mom, we'll see you later." As soon as her mom was out of the room, she slammed her fist down on the table and ranted, "Okay, what is it? Talk to me. Say what you gotta say! Are you freaked out that I'm a lesbian?"

"I didn't call you that. I would never call you that," I said.

"I call myself that, Randal." She laughed. "I wonder if you're a homophobe. Are you, Randal?"

"I didn't know you were gay if that's what you're saying. Are you gay? I'm confused because we haven't had this talk," I said. Becca nodded. "When did you change? When did you go all boyish on me? And why didn't you tell me? You act like it's my fault that I'm not comfortable. I have a choice as to the type of people I hang around."

"I'm the same person, Randal. I haven't changed," Becca defended.

"Oh, you changed tremendously, Becca. Quit trying to make me uncomfortable! I'm trying to

adjust here," I said, happy I found a voice to tell her what I really thought.

She was actually taken aback by my tough stance. Maybe she was evaluating my comments too harshly. I said I was trying to adjust to her being gay, not trying to adjust to seeing if I was gay. She started squinting, like I had insulted her. At that moment, I was all confused.

"Look, look, Becca, I don't wanna argue with you. And I'm certainly not trying to judge you. We are different and that's okay. Heck, I got a lot on my plate already trying to figure out who I am. When and how you changed is your business."

"No, no, I care about you, Randal, and I don't want you looking at me like I got some disease. I'm gay and I'm proud of it. Took me awhile to own up to that fact, but once I did, I've never been more free. I've never felt more liberated. I've never felt better in my own skin," Becca said.

I wanted to say, "Bravo to you. Isn't that just great! You know who you are. Yay!" However, I didn't want to sound sarcastic. I really didn't know what to say. I felt afraid to encourage her. So I just looked at her with a questioning face.

Without any comment from me, she started explaining, "See, most guys are after just one thing and not really trying to be there and care. Our friendship—yours and mine—back in the day, was strong. It was intense. It was real. It was deep and awesome. When you have that kind of connection with someone, it's only natural that things become physical. You can't be that open with guys. All they think about is sports, cars, and sex."

What? Feeling her theory didn't hold up, I interjected. "I have several girlfriends who have really good boyfriends. So your philosophy doesn't hold up in my experience."

Becca laughed. "Your experience ... do you have a boyfriend? Are you actually in those relationships? Do you know exactly what's going on? People tell you they are happy all the time, but that doesn't actually mean they're happy, Randal Raines. C'mon."

Shoot, she had a point. Charli couldn't be a hundred percent happy with Brenton because she leaned toward Blake some days. I thought, "But Amir bent over backwards for Hallie, and Leo was a former player till he dove head first

into a relationship with Ella. Certainly, those things weren't fake. Everything there had to be real."

"You're pondering what I'm saying, huh? As real as a girl-guy relationship may seem, it can't be as intense as a girl-girl relationship. I'm just saying you don't need to knock it till you try it."

"I'm fine, thank you," I snapped. Wow, I needed to watch what was going on here. I didn't want to be rude, but I had to get this girl to understand that I was not interested in her lifestyle.

"Like my mom," Becca said, still trying to convince me. "She's in a relationship with my dad, but she's never happier than when she goes out with her girlfriends. Now she's not trying to kiss on them or anything, but she's got some feeling that only makes her happy when she spends time with the girls."

"You're reaching, Becca. You're trying to justify a rationale for who you are and why you are this way."

"No, you're completely misunderstanding me. I'm very fine with who I am, but you're just reaching to find out who you are. I was just trying to say, don't miss out on something that can

be beautiful. I can't tell what's going on with you, Randal, but I know it's something heavy. I reached out to you because I've been thinking about you."

Please, please, don't have her say she likes me like that. Although her actions were showing it earlier, I did not need to hear her verify it. Hopefully, that public comment was to make Savannah jealous. I saw her kissing somebody else. Even if I was into girls, certainly she didn't think I wanted to share. But I wasn't into girls. All of this was just crazy.

"I ... I don't wanna talk anymore," I abruptly said.

"I'm not trying to stress you out," she said. She came over and played with my curly hair. When she stroked my cheek, there was actually something about it that relaxed me. It was like when I was with ER earlier in the evening and my heart skipped a few beats. Now Becca's touch was sending chills up my spine.

What was really going on with me? Why was I so fragile? In the quest to find myself, I was swaying in too many directions. I took a step back from Becca, inhaled and exhaled.

I grabbed the towel that Becca's mom had left for me and said, "Excuse me, I need to use the bathroom."

Having time alone, I felt sick. It seemed like my world was spinning out of control, and I desperately needed to get it to stop twirling. How was that possible when so many different things were affecting me? I didn't know, but I had to find the answers, so the search continued.

Thankfully, we had regional competition. My mom came and got me from Becca's early the next morning. It was so early that Becca was still sleeping. That was fine with me. I didn't want her to talk to me. I didn't want her to repeat what she said the night before. I didn't want her to look at me. I just wanted to get out of her place.

In the car, when my mom asked me if I had a good time, I said, "Please, tell me about overnight plans before you agree to let me stay with anybody!"

"What are you talking about, Randal? Becca is your best friend," my mother said, having no clue about what was going on with Becca.

"Mom, I haven't see her since *middle school*. I'm a junior, and I think you might want to see her before you assume she's the same sweet little girl you remember."

"What are you talking about, Randal?"

"Forget it, Mom," I sighed.

"I'm so glad you got your buddy back," she said. Changing the subject, she mused, "I raised you well. You're so organized, honey. I picked up your cheer bag and found everything you texted for me to pick up. I'm going to drop you off at Lockwood, and then I'll meet you guys at the competition."

"Fine," I said, still completely salty at her for planning my life without permission.

I was in high school. I didn't need her to help with my social life. While I had issues with my besties from Lockwood, I didn't need my mom to make my world right. I simply needed her to get me a debit card with unlimited access and get me my own car so I wouldn't have to depend on anybody. In my dreams I laughed to myself.

When I got to Lockwood, Charli, Hallie, Ella, and Eva were clustered together. They looked at me coldly. While I should have stayed with them,

I wasn't going to beg them to be my friends. Charli was the cheerleading captain. Of all the girls, she should have been the most welcoming. But I wasn't one of her favorite people, and she had no problems letting me know it.

"I can't believe you hung up on me," she scolded as we boarded the bus.

"I can't believe you're the captain and you're holding grudges," I blurted.

"Ladies, let's get on the bus," Coach Woods ordered.

Obeying, we kept it moving. I knew they usually sat in the front, so I kept on going to the back. Whitney, the co-captain, and a high-maintenance cheerleader sat across from me. She was grinning, like I had info as juicy as a good steak to tell her.

Whitney probed, "You guys have so many issues with each other. Last week, Eva wasn't speaking to you guys, and now you're on the outs with everybody. Ugh, with friends like y'all, who needs enemies?"

I wanted to second that, but as mad as I was at my girls, I still cared about them. I was tired of being a wuss, the one they always pushed around.

The one who never had a say. The one who did whatever they wanted to do. The one they took for granted. While they made me feel like I should be happy they were my friends, I was now starting to feel they should be equally happy, if not more so, to have me in their lives as well.

Becca did have a point with female friends and bonds. I cared deeply for my girls. Just because some boys were saying something sweet to them, I was the odd man out. If the tables were reversed, there was no way I would make them feel isolated.

I remembered at one of the first dances of the year, the guys were asking all of us to dance but Hallie. She was standing on the wall, looking all pitiful, and then I told my dance partner to ask her. Even though he didn't want to, I made him. Before he got to her, Amir stepped in. Still, I wasn't trying to leave her out. I detested that my girls didn't have a do-unto-others attitude.

Coach Woods stood before we got off the bus and said, "Ladies, we have put in an awful lot of hard work this semester on our routine. We started off a little rocky, not even placing in some meets, but we tightened up on things, and added

more difficulty to a few of the routines. We're ready. I know there's tension on this bus because it's thick like fog, but when we step out on that floor, the sunshine better be in your hearts so we can all put on a show. Understand?"

No one responded. She repeated herself. She did not let us off until we agreed.

Thirty minutes later that's exactly what we did. We put on a show. Even Ella was excited. She had gotten shot and was unable to perform a couple weeks before, but now that she had healed, she was performing with us, and we were stellar. As soon as we got off the floor, some of our cheerleaders started chanting.

They sang, "Who dat, who dat, who dat think they bad? Lockwood Lions know they bad 'cause we kicked you in your shhh, shhh, shhh."

More Lions cheerleaders joined in. The crowd who came to support us joined in. The black folks were loud. I looked at my mom, and she was looking at our crowd like, *Okay, settle down, people. This is not the time and place. You don't want points taken off because you're being loud and rude and disrespectful.* Basically, she didn't want us to be so ghetto.

I didn't feel comfortable when I noticed other teams looking at us. I also felt a little jealous when I saw my four best girlfriends celebrating together. They didn't compliment my jumps. I did a high, dope basket toss. I had to be my own cheerleader, and that honestly angered me. I got up and went to the bathroom and was caught off guard when I ran straight into Jillian.

"Oh my gosh, Randal," Jillian sneered. "You're one of the Lockwood Lions rah-rah girls. Ugh."

Holding my nose up just as high as hers was, I scoffed, "I didn't know *you* were a cheerleader."

"Yeah, because I don't cheer for football. That's lame. That's for the girls who have no skills." I shook my head and she continued, "Oh, you cheer football, right? Well, no worries. Good for you guys. You're gonna qualify, but no way you're going to win state. Your routine is too, ugh … gosh … just like your mannerisms."

"We're too *what*?" I asked through gritted teeth.

"I won't talk about your team. I just don't know how you could do it. How could you stand

it? How could you want to be a Lockwood Lion and not stay at Grovehill? I mean, you're dynamic. That basket toss was so high; it was like you had no fear. Ours was good, but the girl we got who goes up … let's just say you beat her."

"We added more complexity to our routine. I don't know if you saw the whole thing," I explained, believing that would change her position on how pitiful she thought we were compared to the rest of the teams.

"Oh, I saw it all. We watch everybody, and we always laugh at Lockwood. While you guys have gotten better since the last competition, you're still way below the top-notch talent in this state. You're totally undisciplined. You don't all walk in together. Your uniforms look sloppy, and none of your gear is uniform. A couple of the girls chew gum while they perform. Your motions aren't tight. While your dance moves have energy, they have no true style. It's like everybody is shaking their rear. Ya'll just scream out g-h-e-t-t-o, don't you think? 'Who dat, who dat,' " Jillian pitifully mocked. "This is not a basketball game. All you guys are going to be kicking yourselves when you go to state and get embarrassed."

"Yeah, maybe you have a point," I said half-heartedly.

"Well, you better tell *them*," Jillian nodded toward the door.

As I turned around, my mouth hung open. Hallie and Ella were in the doorway. I had just agreed with Jillian because I wanted her to hush up and get out. Okay, maybe a part of me did sort of agree that my squad needed to settle down and not act so black in a white sport. I didn't want drama. Now, I had probably caused World War III when all I wanted to do was reduce stress.

CHAPTER 3

Rattle Things

Good luck at state," Jillian snarked to Hallie and Ella, brushing by them. " 'Cause you're gonna need it. Bye, Randal, let me know if you wanna come back to Grovehill and try out for our classy team."

I wanted to shout *get out* at the top of my lungs! Mean stares and harsh looks were being shot my way by Hallie and Ella. Their intense tension made me stay quiet.

"Why were you even talking about us?" Hallie barked.

"I wasn't talking about you guys," I asserted.

"Yeah, right," Ella said. "What, you think we're dummies?"

"No," Hallie said. "She thinks we're ghetto, too black, and straight from Watts Road. We're an embarrassment."

Ella said, "We came in here to get you because our moms are planning to take us to lunch to celebrate."

"I don't know when you guys walked in here, but you only heard part of the conversation," I said, needing them to not jump to conclusions.

"Save it, Randal Raines," Ella ordered. "We been through a lot as girlfriends—"

"You mean, you guys have been through a lot, and I have always been there. When you guys have a crisis, I'm always right there. But when I go through some things, y'all are the first ones to abandon me. So think what you want. I'm an afterthought for you anyway."

Before they could give a smart comment, I was out of the bathroom. I wanted to find Jillian and strangle her. She set me up. I remembered when she was washing her hands and out of the blue came the conversation bashing my girls. She probably turned on the water after she saw who came in so I wouldn't hear them. She started talking louder, and when I was about to

turn and leave, she touched my shoulder. Ugh, she made me sick.

It was hard to find anybody in the crowd because lots of cheerleaders were exiting the gym, but then I spotted a ton of red and royal blue. I knew that was Grovehill. Surely, Jillian had to be close by, and then I heard yelling.

"This is not gonna work, Jillian, okay? We're through," a familiar male voice said sternly.

I peeked around the corner and saw ER breaking up with Jillian. Her face was bright red. I folded my arms and pleasantly watched the show.

"You don't wanna do that, ER. You don't wanna break up with me. I'm the best thing you got going in your life. You're down there with those gangsters."

"You are a racist, Jillian. I'm tired of it. You're not my wife. You nag me to death. I'm playing again, and I can't be stressed."

"You played a great game on Friday," she said.

"I did okay, but I have to go and watch film so I can get better. We have a playoff game next week. But that's not what we were talking about."

"ER, man, you ready to go?" Landon asked, walking up with Leo.

Both of them were two guys from my school. Jillian looked at the black guys with anger. ER was about to walk away.

Jillian pitifully blurted out, "So you're just going to go? You are just going to leave. You're going to break up with me?"

"What, are you deaf?" I uttered, not even a part of their conversation. I was still hot mad at the girl for putting me in a tough place.

ER left her and came up to me and said, "Hey."

"Hi," I said.

"Don't you even think about going after my boyfriend! We're just having a temporary set-back," Jillian screeched.

"He called you a racist, which I know you are," I hissed.

"Please, he's not that different from me. He's only at your school so he can get a great scholarship. Everybody knows white athletes playing with black guys can get their stock raised up a little. He's not trying to go to Spelman or Howard or any other black college."

"He can't get into Spelman. It's an all-girls school, idiot."

"Randal, there you are," my mom declared. "I've been looking for you, sweetie. We've gotta go. Wow, a Grovehill cheerleader. Do you remember Randal?"

"Oh yes, ma'am, I do. We miss her terribly in East Cobb. Our favorite sista is gone," Jillian said, trying to be sweet and snide.

The whole racist remark went over my mom's head. I wanted to smack Jillian, but at the moment I needed my mom to understand that we weren't going to anybody's luncheon. Before I could tell her that, Charli's mom was walking beside us.

Mrs. Black said, "Randal, you girls did so well. Third place in your region qualifies you for state."

"Yes, ma'am," I said.

"I know everybody's tired. We are just going to get a quick bite to eat to celebrate," Mrs. Black said, sensing I wanted to avoid their plans.

"Yeah, girl time," my mom said, sounding real white and corny.

Since the regional competition was down-town at the World Congress Center, we went

right around the corner to a restaurant called Pascal's. Though my mom was a caterer, soul food was not her thing to prepare. She loved eating it, but she really could not make it. Her fried chicken was always a little burnt. Her mac and cheese was never creamy. Her yams weren't good because she thought the recipes had too much butter, so she used yogurt instead. Who liked low-fat yams?

So as we sat at a round table for ten, she criticized the menu. "I just don't see how you guys can eat this stuff continually. Everything has so much fat in it."

"I know, girl, but it's good," Ms. Blount, the twins' mom said.

I was actually surprised that their new stepmom, Samantha, was with us too. She and Eva appeared to have made amends, but I knew nothing about it. Hallie lived with her father and her mom was in rehab, but her dad was now dating a lady named Greta. She was there too. She and Hallie were real chummy, which was good to see. I knew Hallie wanted her mom, but it seemed she was softening to the idea of her father having a girlfriend. Thanksgiving was

right around the corner, and the ladies started talking about the meals they were going to prepare. When they began talking about chitlins, my mom seemed like a fish out of water.

She said, "My husband wants to eat those, but I just refuse to cook pig intestines. How do you eat them?"

"Oh, girl, with some hot sauce," Ms. Blount laughed.

"If you don't fix good soul food, how do you keep that man of yours happy?" Greta asked.

"I know! Right?" Ms. Blount said. The rest of them also agreed.

Mom defended, "I just tell him we can't have all of that, and he goes for it."

The four black women looked at each other. My mom shrugged her shoulders, not caring. She didn't fix any greasy, fatty, or unhealthy foods. My dad went for whatever she said.

"Ladies, y'all know white women got something that makes black men lose their minds," Samantha chuckled.

Maybe they weren't picking on my mom, but it felt like it. Or maybe I was just paranoid. Either way, I certainly was dead on about the looks

I was getting from my girls. It was like the four of them wanted to be anywhere but sitting at the table with me.

Without being able to hold back the tears, I just stood up and said, "Mom, can we go, please?"

"We're not finished celebrating with your friends," she said, picking the ham hocks out of the greens.

"Friends? They're not my friends. They hate me," I uttered.

Charli's mom looked at her. "I know they don't."

The twins' mom looked at her girls. "Yeah, I know they don't."

"You better go," Hallie said to me. " 'Cause I don't think you want us to tell everyone what happened in the bathroom."

My mom wouldn't get up. "I want to know what happened. Randal loves you girls. Surely there's a misunderstanding."

"Mom, can we go? They think I'm a racist, okay?" I barked.

"Randal, what are you talking about? Where would they get an idea like that? How could you be racist? You're black."

"There you go, Mom. You finally said it. Even *you* don't think I'm white when half of me is the same color you are. I hate my life! I hate my skin! And I hate who I am!" I vented. I jetted out of Pascal's as fast as my feet would take me.

"Randal, you need to go back in there right now and apologize," my mom ordered. She was near the car and was making a grab for my arm.

"Unlock the car, Mom. I'm doing no such thing."

"Are you sassing me?"

"I'm not trying to be disrespectful. I'm just not going to go in there and apologize. Please, can we go? Please, can you just listen to me? I'm your daughter, Mom, and I don't want to be here right now. I don't wanna cause a scene, and I don't wanna be here when they come outside. Can you honor that, *please*?" I begged.

"Fine! I can't believe you embarrassed me like that, Randal. I raised you to—"

Angrily, I cut her off and spat, "To what? Be a sweet girl? To go along to get along? To care about the next person's feelings more than I care about my own? To blend in to any situation? To

not really rock the boat? Yes, Mom, you're right. That's exactly how you raised me. Congratulations, you did an outstanding job, but who am I really? Who is your daughter if I never have my own voice? If I never speak my own mind? Or if I never stand up to people who wrong me?" Seeing her look dumbfounded, I got even more frustrated. "You know what? I don't even know why I'm trying to get you to understand. We're on two different freaking planets."

"Watch your mouth," she threatened.

"What did I say that's so wrong, Mom?"

Shaking her head, she unlocked the doors. "What has gotten into you?" she asked.

"What do you mean?"

Finally, she started up the car. Thankfully, we were getting out of there. "I just don't know who you are, Randal. I don't know where all of this is coming from. This hostility and animosity and sheer aggression you have toward me."

"Mom, what I'm feeling has nothing to do with you. I mean, I have nothing against you. If it's all the same, I'd just rather not say anything."

At that point, she abruptly swooped into the other entrance of Pascal's parking lot. "Do I need

to park right in front of the restaurant for you to decide you want to talk?"

"No, Mom! No, no, no, no," I said in a panic when I saw Charli and the crew coming out. "Please, let's go. I'll talk."

She sure knew how to get under my skin.

"Will you just talk to me, baby?" she pleaded. Her tone let me know that she really did want to know what was going on with me.

However, how could I articulate it to her when I'd been trying not to focus on it myself? I was sick with questions. I had so much pent-up anger that I was afraid to let out.

"Promise me you won't freak out," I said.

"I won't, baby, just talk to me."

"I'm having self-esteem issues, okay?"

"What do you mean? You're a beautiful girl."

"Mom, beauty is only skin deep. I don't know whether I'm coming or going."

"I don't understand."

"Mom, I don't know if I'm black or white."

"You're both, baby. You know that."

"That's not true, Mom. If you were honest with yourself, you wouldn't even consider me white."

"What are you talking about?" she asked, making me go there. "Mom, you wish my hair was like yours."

"Your hair is cute."

"Mom, I heard you saying that to your friend years ago, so don't deny it."

"Well, that's just because I didn't know how to take care of it. Trust me, I'm very thankful that you don't have to wash your hair every day like me. There are pros and cons to everything. Baby, I think you're perfect just the way you are."

"Well, Mom, I don't. I've heard it a bunch of times. Anytime you got a little bit of chocolate mixed with the cream, then you're not a pure-bred white person. We even have relatives who feel that way about me, Mom. Your mom doesn't think I'm white enough, and Dad's mom doesn't think I'm black enough."

"They are set in their ways, sweetheart."

"So is that supposed to make me feel better? Didn't my own grandfather disown you 'cause you married Dad? Oh, and don't think it's any better on his side of the family. I get a whole bunch of looks over there, like they think that I

think I'm better than everybody 'cause I am half white. They think I think I'm too good for them and that I talk too white."

"You don't have a horrible life, Randal. Nowadays everybody is mixed with a little something."

"Not you, not Dad."

"At your school?"

"Mom, please, at my school people call me cracker behind my back. When I was in East Cobb they said: You're light but don't get it twisted, you're not white, as if I was trying to pass myself off as something that I wasn't. I don't have low self-esteem, Mom, I have no self-esteem."

"Oh, Randal, sweetheart," she reached out and stroked my hair.

"Mom, I don't want you to think a hug and a kiss is gonna make it better, 'cause even you have issues with the life you've chosen."

"Your dad and I might disagree on a lot of cultural things, but I have *no* regrets. I wouldn't change a thing."

"Mom, you're lying."

"Randal!"

"Mom, I'm sorry. I just don't believe you, okay? I see you uncomfortable in church. When black people get really excited, you squirm because you want a more settled, quick, or relaxed church service. Then you go to the white church service, but you hate all the looks you get about your black husband. I just know you're uncomfortable."

"You're seeing what you want to see," my mom muttered.

"Tell me I'm not seeing things from your perspective, Mom? Be honest with me and tell me I'm wrong. You can't."

"I think you have the best of both worlds."

"The problem is, Mom, I don't fit in anywhere. And I've been so focused trying to fit in somewhere that I didn't ask myself where I wanna be. Thanksgiving is coming up, and I heard you and Dad going on and on about whose house we're going to. Well, can we just stay at our house for once?"

"You know we have to make our rounds, Randal. Don't make this difficult."

"But when I go, it's difficult for *me*. I wanna be comfortable for once. And happy. But I'm so

far from happy. I'm starting to hate everybody. I give and give and give to all the people in my life. Whatever anybody wants me to do, I do it. I'm tired of being used. You'd think people would return the favor, but nobody seems to care about helping me. Everybody's got their own agenda, and they only do what's best for them. Forget about Randal. Forget about her feelings. Nobody even tries to understand me or what I'm going through. I wish I was dead."

Giant tears flowed down my mom's face. I didn't mean to say such harsh things to my mom. I knew it hurt her. But the truth was the truth.

"Mom, don't cry. I'm not planning to go kill myself or anything like that," I said, hoping to stop her sobbing.

"How am I supposed to take this? You think I'm supposed to be happy hearing what you are saying. You hate your life! You wish you were dead! Randal, you're my baby. I don't want you to have pain."

"But you can't protect me from everything either, Mom. I'm telling you, I have to figure out my life."

"You do know your dad and I love you, right?"

"I do, Mom, but I gotta love myself. I gotta be happy with me, and right now I'm not."

She pulled over into a gas station and gave me a gigantic hug. "I can't pretend that I understand what you're going through. Though you're right, and if I'm honest with myself, my life may have been easier if I married a white man, but I married for love. I married for joy. I longed to be happy. And admit it, your father is a stud. Whatever we need to do to make sure you feel happy, consider it done. Do you remember what I used to tell you when you were a little girl?" she asked.

"You're somebody special. You're beautiful. You're my daughter whom I love. Yes, I remember, Mom. Now, I just gotta love me."

"Don't worry, you will," she said, kissing my brow. "You will."

Because she cared that much about me, maybe I would find a way out of this dark hole. Finally, she was understanding. I had light in the midst of my gloom. She was my light. She wasn't going to let me stay down. I was happy about that, but I was still feeling down.

Though I hated to admit it, going to school and walking through the halls without my girls was no fun. It was almost the end of the first semester of our junior year. Christmas, New Year's, Valentine's Day, and prom were just around the corner. Looking at Eva and Ella walking with their new guys made me feel self-conscious.

Everybody had paired up so quickly in the last few months, except me. I was still alone. What was wrong with me? Why wasn't I with anybody? Then I felt somebody touch my waist.

"I see the way your lips are creamy, wanting someone to kiss them like your girls got going on over there," the sleazy male voice belted out.

I tried to jerk away from the guy's funky breath, but he had a hold of my belt loop. "What are you doing?" I turned to see that it was Waxton.

"I been peeping you out for a while," he said, trying to lick my ear.

"Ew, stop! What are you doing?" I said to him again in disgust.

"Calm down. I think you and me need to be an item. I've seen the way you've been looking at me, and it's your lucky day 'cause now I want you too."

"I'm trying to get to class. I don't know what you think you know about what I want, but you're way off the mark."

"Nobody tells Wax no, baby," he uttered. He tugged on me a little harder, like I was a dog on a leash.

I was really confused 'cause we just went through this whole thing. Our school had two separate assemblies about sexual violence. I don't know what they talked about in the one the boys had, but in our girls' session, we covered when a girl says *no*, she means *no*. I didn't want any beef or drama. I certainly didn't have any girls to back me up, but I wasn't gonna let this guy grope me.

I screamed, "Stop!"

He raised his hand like he wanted to slap me. I squinted in fear. Suddenly, ER grabbed his hand, and Eva was standing by my side.

"What do you think you're doing?" Eva said to Waxton, surprising me.

He yelled, "Go on back over there. Ain't nobody even talking to you. Go back and make another video."

"Oh. No. You. Didn't," Eva spat.

"Wait a minute, Wax. What's up, man? You don't need to be disrespecting her like that," Landon butted in.

Wax shouted, "Please, just because you ain't dipping in the sauce doesn't mean it ain't messy. And, ER, boy, get your hands off of me."

When Landon balled his fist to swing at Waxton, Leo pulled him away. "He ain't even worth it, man. He ain't even worth it."

"White boy, what you gonna do?" Waxton challenged.

"I'm not going to let you take what somebody's not giving you," ER threatened, tightening the grip.

"Please, dude with no appropriate name, in a minute somebody gonna have to take you to the emergency room if you don't get your hand off me."

"I'm just trying to get you to settle down," ER said.

"What do you care who I talk to?"

Waxton wrestled himself from ER's grip, and the two of them stood toe to toe. Everybody knew Waxton thought he ruled the school. As a senior and arguably the best football player

on the team, nobody really challenged him. I've been sheltered most of my upbringing. And I didn't know a lot about a lot, but he looked high. He was all jittery, and his eyes were bugged out.

"Are you okay?" Eva turned and said while the guys tussled and shoved each other back and forth.

"I can't believe you care," I cried.

"Girl, please," Eva said, nudging me. "You know you my girl."

"Yeah, but I'm sure your sister told you what she thought I said."

"What she thought you said? Or what you really said?" Eva asked, unsure I was telling the truth. "Ella's your biggest cheerleader. She don't never put any words in your mouth. You're ashamed of the crazy black people. That's your prerogative."

I actually couldn't believe I was hearing her say those words.

"Talk to me, Randal. What's been going on with you, girl?" Eva asked.

She was really concerned about me. I so totally wanted to grab her hand, go into the girls restroom, and just pour my heart out. However,

the crowd got louder as the boys were about to take the drama up another notch.

"I didn't want anybody getting in trouble. I surely didn't want ER out here fighting," I said. Eva and I stepped in the center of the gathering crowd.

"Ahh, he's coming to your rescue mighty hard," she told me, as we both saw serious determination on ER's face.

Knowing he had a girlfriend, I said, "Don't make anything of it."

"No, I'm serious. ER was really upset that Wax was trying to come on to you. I know because he was standing with Landon and me in the hall. He was eyeing you before Wax even put his hand where it wasn't supposed to go. You know what I'm saying?"

Dismissing her theory, I said, "Thank you for standing by me."

Eva kept it real as always. "Girl, I'm not mad at you. I've been dealing with my own drama."

I nodded and empathized. "I know, I know. You're still getting over what happened to you."

It was crazy to think that Eva was raped. I say crazy because she was the strongest female

I knew. Sometimes even when your guard is up, people can still break you down. I knew it was gonna take a lot to heal, and I was actually thankful that she had Landon to help her.

Another scandal broke out at the same time as the video of Eva's rape floated around. We all found out that Landon had been molested by his little league football coach years ago. Recently, the man came back as a substitute teacher at Lockwood High School. Basically, everything hit the fan.

Both situations were tragic, so it was great that Eva and Landon could help each other. I got nervous when I looked over at ER, hoping he wouldn't get his face smashed in. I naturally assumed Waxton could take him if he wanted, but it appeared Waxton was all talk. When he said the wrong thing, ER punched him. Waxton went running down the hall.

"My nose! My nose is broke," he hollered.

There appeared to be blood, but I doubted his nose was broken. People were giving ER dap. I could tell he didn't want all the praise. I tried to thank him, but people shouted as the crowd broke up.

I heard folks screaming, "Dr. Sapp is coming. Get to class."

Eva and I started moving. Dr. Sapp eyed us down like he suspected we were a part of the chaos. Dr. Sapp headed straight over to Eva.

"Dang it," she said, trying to walk around him, but he would not let her. "Sir, I'm not a magnet for trouble."

"What's going on, Miss Blount? Talk to me," he asked, not buying her story.

"I don't know, sir," she said. She motioned for Landon to take ER and go.

Dr. Sapp asked, "You don't know, huh?"

"Nope."

"Do you know?" he asked me. "All this commotion in the hall; sounded like a fight to me."

"I don't know, sir," I said, needing no problems with the head man at our school. I remembered Ella's in-school suspension a few weeks back, and I did not want that happening to me.

"It's just the football players fooling around. Everybody's hyped because we're undefeated."

"Didn't look like y'all were getting along down here to me," he said sternly. I knew he was trying to make me to flinch.

I noticed that ER was looking back at me from down the hall. Again, I had a strong desire to thank him. I guess the intensity of my glare got the message through because he smiled my way.

"The boys are just too hyped, sir," Eva stated. "You better tell them to settle down and save it all for the field. We got a big game Friday night and—"

"You're reading my mind. I wouldn't want anybody to get suspended or expelled. If that happened, they would be off the team. That would certainly mess up our championship hopes and rattle things."

CHAPTER 4

Ludicrous Feelings

On our way to our away game, playing Grovehill High, I had the craziest thoughts. I knew it was not just going to be a game. I felt something was going to go wrong. I hated feeling that way. I hated thinking my life was about to be messed up before it even played out, but I couldn't shake what I was thinking.

Trying not to get worked up, I chilled in the back seat and listened to music on iTunes. This game didn't really mean anything to us. Since we hadn't lost all season, we were going to have home-field advantage.

However, our football coach didn't want us going into the playoffs with a loss. I knew that because we had a pep rally and that's exactly what Coach Strong said. He told us we needed to keep the momentum swinging in our favor.

Grovehill had a lot to play for. They were eight and one, and they wanted to get home-field advantage. To get another win under their belt would secure that.

I was so torn when I saw tons of cars following us in a caravan to East Cobb. On one hand, I wanted no one follow us to the game as we had a tendency to bring loud fans who were the opposite of the boojie ones from Grovehill. I so hoped there would be no ruckus. However, I didn't want the Lions to lose. So I knew, even at an away game, we needed the twelfth man.

"I'll be glad when this game is over and we're on our way home," I mumbled to myself, feeling isolated.

Hallie sat a few seats up from me on the bus and talked to Charli and Ella. I knew they hoped the team won because on the ride home the cheerleaders would be able to sit with the football players. On the way up there, however,

it was all business. Coach Strong didn't allow any fraternizing, and it surely didn't matter to me either way. I was alone on the ride up, and I knew I would be alone on the ride back.

Eva and I were cool again, thankfully. We weren't chatting it up, though. She seemed to be in her own funk, which only made sense. If you were raped, no one could expect you to get over it immediately.

While I missed my girls terribly, I tried hard as I could not to let it phase me. I did not want the other three talking about how pitiful I was. Besides, if we were supposed to be such good friends, I didn't need to be the one reaching out all the time.

Honestly, I had forgotten why we weren't speaking. Oh yeah, they had accused me of being a racist. I was accusing them of being fair-weather friends. They should know me better than that. I've always stuck my head out there to calm the waters and lessen the drama. They should know I wasn't trying to make it murky and stir things up.

A part of me believed what Jillian was saying at the regional competition. My girls were extra

loud sometimes. That did not mean I thought less of them. I did not help make amends when I stepped off the bus and walked smack into the Grovehill cheerleaders and Jillian. She was all smiles, coming up to me trying to give me the biggest hug. Seeing Charli almost dare me to open up to Jillian, I backed away.

"Oh, so it's like that, Randal?" Jillian said, when I left her hanging. Charli and the crew walked onto our team's side, leaving me and Eva.

"We just came over to let you girls know where the facilities are."

"We don't need a tour guide to tell us where the bathroom is," Eva said bluntly.

"Well, excuse us," Jillian sneered and stomped off.

Before I could follow my squad to the visitor's side, three other cheerleaders I knew from middle school swarmed me.

"How have you been, Randal?" a girl name Kristy asked.

I remembered her vividly; she looked beautiful now. She had lost a tooth when she fell off a bicycle, but apparently that was all fixed. Now she was with glamour girls, Parker and

Rona. They were always popular and looked like two Barbie dolls with gorgeous flowing blonde hair, blue eyes, and bodies with curves that always made them look more mature than they were. They weren't sisters, but they looked like clones.

"Why is Jillian cheering?" I asked them. "I though she didn't cheer for football."

Kristy said, "Two of our girls are out, and Coach just let some of the competition girls cheer. One has pneumonia and one has mono."

Just hearing the word *mono*, my face held a mortified glare. Instantly, I thought of Becca dabbling in a little bit of everything. People really needed to be careful.

"I know, right?" Parker said. She confirmed I wasn't the only one who thought it was icky.

Rona added, "Since everybody kisses everybody around here, a bunch of people went to their doctors to get treated." I stayed and chatted with the three of them for a little while. They walked me back over to my side.

Charli yelled at me, "We didn't come here to hang out with friends. This is war! We've all been warming up, and you've been socializing."

"It's not like we're the football team, Charli," I defended. I sure was sick and tired of taking her crap. "Just because I have old friends here doesn't mean I'm not rooting for the Lions. You act like I know the coach's playbook and I'm giving away trade secrets or something. Slow your roll! You're the cheerleading captain, not my freaking mama."

"Yeah, we've all seen how you respect her, getting up and leaving a restaurant when she is trying to talk to you. You're such a—" Charli said, stopping herself, as if trying to find the right words.

I could tell she wanted to make a smart-mouth comment. I just put up my hand and walked away. It was clear I'd lost my best friends. Before I could even process the thought that I was relieved that Eva and me were still cool, something weird happened. Lots of folks from Grovehill came over to our side, and people were pointing at her, looking at their phones, and laughing. It didn't take any time for us to figure out what was going on. Somehow, some-way, someone had gotten a hold of *that* video. I was shocked when Eva rushed over to me and pushed me hard. I fell to the ground.

"What the heck, Eva!" I jumped up and yelled.

"You are a trip. Here I am feeling all sorry for you, standing up for you. Then you go and betray me."

"What are you talking about?" I asked.

Eva pointed toward the people. Even the cheerleaders who I was just with were part of the gawking crew. Some folks were even mouthing for me to call them. It seemed like I sent the video, but I did not. I was really upset that they were making fun of Eva. I'd never sell her out like that.

She insisted it was me. "You told them! There is no way these people would have known about the video unless you said something about it. I *know* it was you!"

Tears filled my eyes. However, I refused to let them flow. I turned them off and kept my sadness, anger, and frustration to myself.

Turning to Eva, I said, "Believe what you want to believe."

She huffed. I huffed back. We went on to cheer for our team, but the tension was horrible.

Thankfully, we won the game. It could not have been over quick enough for me. You know it's bad when the sophomore cheerleaders don't

want to have anything to do with you. Ella, Charli, and Hallie were all too excited to console Eva, practically telling her that they told her not to mess with me.

"Randal's a traitor. You see why we're not friends with her now, don't you?" Charli barked.

I was so happy when the four of them sat on the first bus. My inward smile faded when Becca and her pals came up to me before I could get on the second bus.

"You cheered really well," she complimented. Then she touched my hair in that creepy way.

I yanked it away from her and said, "Thanks, I gotta get on the bus. I really gotta go."

"Why are you running away from me? Why are you running away from this feeling?"

I hated to tell her that I wasn't feeling anything, but I didn't wanna have another confrontation this night, so I said, "I'll be in touch, okay?"

"Don't sweat those other girls. They are just jealous," Becca said, clearly showing me she had been watching me.

I got on the bus with a quick step because knowing she was practically stalking me was

gross. I saw ER walking onto the bus and my heartbeat picked up. For some reason, I wanted him to come sit beside me and kiss me hard, but I clearly dismissed the feeling, knowing he was going to sit with a teammate. However, when he kept walking, I got nervous. He stood in front of me, and our eyes met.

"You mind if I sit with you?" he asked.

I wanted to ask him about Jillian and how the two of them were doing. Why did he want to sit with me when there were plenty of other seats? Coach Woods told everyone to sit down so we could take off. Without answering his question, I slid over.

"Great game," I complimented.

"Yeah, thanks," he quipped in a monotone voice.

Hmm, his tone wasn't as peppy as I thought it should be. "Now it's time to concentrate on the big one," I said.

"Yup, playoffs, here we come."

"It had to feel good kicking the ball through the uprights."

"Not when I started the game off missing the first kick, but in the end it felt real good.

I didn't wanna let my team down. Bigger game next week, though."

I just wanted to take ER's hand and hold it. Not because I had growing feelings for him, but because when we talked about the upcoming game, he was shaking. He was nervous. I could tell he was scared. I wanted to help him through it. What could I do?

The last place I wanted to be going to was the state cheerleading championship, which was horrible because I had been practicing for the event practically half the year. We had to leave Atlanta and drive in cars for ninety minutes down to Columbus, Georgia, spend the night, and then perform. The goal was to be a finalist, but we had to qualify first. Everything was riding on our first performance.

We were blown out earlier this year in a few different competitions. We qualified to compete in the state meet, but just barely. Some of my fellow cheerleaders weren't thinking rationally when it came to our chances. Charli, Hallie, and Ella were going on and on about how they felt we were going to do so well.

"All we gotta do is execute, and we're gonna show them," Charli pronounced with confidence before we loaded up and headed out.

Cheerleaders could not drive on their own to competitions out of town. I did not want to ride with Charli's mom and the rest of the crew—not that they were inviting me. So I rode with Coach Woods. Everybody else thought she was getting nosy. To me she was so cool and really seemed to care. She did have good perception. She could tell there was a big rift between me and my girls. She asked me about it. I didn't want to reveal anything because I did not want this black lady, who I admired, to view me differently. What if I explained my position and she took their side?

She persisted, "So you don't want to talk about it, Randal? The five of you have been like peas in a pod. Yesterday all your buddies were on a different bus on the way home. I can tell the relationship is strained. And I don't only want to resolve it so we can do well at this competition."

She could tell that was what I was think-ing. Any good cheerleading coach knew that if there was any drama among the girls, they wouldn't compete as well. The flyers, which was

my position, couldn't trust the bases to catch them, thus making the stunts horrible, resulting in bad scores and not moving on to the final round. I just looked away. I didn't want to talk. I hoped she would drop it. She didn't.

Keeping one had on the steering wheel, she touched my shoulder with the other and preached, "High school years fly by. I don't want you to regret petty disagreements that keep you from your friends."

I wondered why she wasn't having this talk with them. Just because I was the one in the minority, as it was four against one, didn't mean it was my fault. It did not mean I needed to be the one to crawl back to them. It didn't mean that I needed to be the one to fix this.

"It's more complicated than a silly disagreement," I uttered, needing my coach and mentor to understand my plight.

"Okay, then talk to me."

"They don't understand me. They don't get me, and truly, I think they don't care. I have always been the one to allow things to go everybody else's way. I thought we were great friends. That's what it felt like to me, but it also felt like

I was the only one giving. That just doesn't sit right with me anymore. If I have to go through this last year and a half without them, then so be it. I will still have my sanity."

"Okay, I hear you talking. While all that sounds all good in theory, I know it won't feel good playing it out. You guys have been too close. Some people's personalities make them more vocal than others, but that doesn't mean the quiet one is less valued—maybe misunderstood, but surely appreciated."

"Maybe I'll write a novel or something, where everything has a happy ending, but not in my real world," I hinted.

Thankfully, she left it alone after that. Riding with my head back, it was extremely hard to come to the realization that my close friendships were over. When we got to the hotel in Columbus, we had five rooms with two queen beds in each. That meant four girls to a room, which was paid for by the dues we had to pay at the beginning of the year. We always knew there were five of us. We would talk about still making sure that we weren't separated. Now that it was actually here, it was all too easy for the four of them to

grab their keys and leave me standing without a place to lay my head.

Whitney, our high-maintenance co-captain, called out, "Wait a minute, Charli, Hallie, Ella, and Eva. Y'all turn around and take this girl. You guys told me I was having my own bed. The five of you were supposed to share. I'm not sleeping with Randal. I don't even know her like that."

Coach Woods stepped in and reprimanded, "You don't have a choice, Whitney."

"It's bad enough as a senior that I gotta share a room with two sophomores. Now I gotta share a bed. Ugh," Whitney pouted, as if sharing a bed with her was what I had longed for.

The night was horrible. Whitney put pillows between us like I had the cooties. I wanted to tell her off and yell that I didn't wanna be around her, either. However, I just dealt with it.

I was so happy when the next morning came. I had aches and pains all over my body from sleeping crazy thanks to Whitney taking more than her share of the bed. I was trying not to be depressed. I was trying not to be upset. I was trying not to want to die, but it didn't feel good being isolated in no man's land.

Actually, I didn't trust any of the heifers on the squad. Eva and Ella didn't want to base me, but we didn't have time to switch positions. Not that I wished it on us, but like I predicted, we were horrible. When it was time to perform, our formations were off, our jumps weren't high, and of course, our stunts fell.

When we got off the floor, the girls stared at me like it was my fault. Upset, I dashed to the bathroom. I didn't wanna hear them complaining or saying it was my fault. All of us owned that pitiful performance. I was gonna be dog-goned on if they were going to blame me. The bottom line: all the hostility we had toward each other off the field showed on the mats.

"You guys ever practice?" Jillian smirked, bumping straight into me as she exited a stall.

"I don't have time for this, please. Leave me alone," I snapped.

"Don't get mad at me because y'all suck."

"Excuse me," I barked, trying to get her to fully understand she had the wrong one on the wrong day.

"Now look, girl," she threatened, "don't go all sista on me. I know you have the spunk in

you because you're around all the black people. Problem is, you think you're white, but you're not. You're just as black as everybody else over there at Lockwood—except for ER of course, and he's about to transfer back. He realizes *that* school is not for him."

I looked at her and actually processed what she was saying. For some reason, I cared about what ER thought. For some reason, I didn't want him to leave me and go back to Grovehill. For some reason, I felt like he and I were connecting. I guess I was wrong.

I was definitely wrong when she said, "And just so you know, I saw you looking at him at the game yesterday. Back off. ER is mine. Yeah, he told me he felt all pitiful for you. Little ole Randal doesn't know where to fit it. I understand you're a mixed-up mess. Well, my beau is not gonna help you get things straight, so leave him alone, loser."

She opened up the door and left. I quickly turned on the water faucet and cupped my hands underneath it. I splashed water all over my face. I could barely breathe. Jillian had my number. I felt so worthless, and all I wanted to

feel was good. Was that possible? At that point, I'd try anything. I desperately wanted some type of relief.

There was no relief, however. When I got home, I saw Becca sitting in my family room chatting it up with my mom. It was so weird because she actually looked more girlie than I had seen her the last couple of times, like she was trying to snow my mom or something.

"There you are, Randal," my mom said. "I heard you guys didn't do too well. Charli's mom texted me."

I guess it wasn't all bad. My mom hadn't lost her friendship with Mrs. Black because we girls had fallen out. Though I could just see Charli, Hallie, and Eva being all mean, telling her mom not to even touch base with mine. That would be beyond. We were at odds, and that wasn't changing no matter how much our mothers talked.

Becca stood to hug me. I did not say a word to her. Fuming, I walked straight into the kitchen; my mom followed me.

"Why are you being rude? Do you see Becca standing there?"

"Mom, why is she here? Why didn't you give me a warning? I don't want any company. Like you said, we did horribly."

"What's done is done, sweetie. I'm not going to let you wallow this whole weekend; besides, her mom and dad had an impromptu trip. They didn't want to leave her alone. When they asked me if it was okay for Becca to spend the night, I said okay. I knew you would enjoy hanging out with her. I realize there has been a little difficulty between you and your friends. This way you would have one friend and wouldn't have to worry about being alone, wallowing in self-pity this weekend," my mom admitted, thinking she was helping me.

"Okay. Well, I'm not for this, so now that you know that, you need to call her mom and tell her she's driving back home or something, 'cause she's not staying with me. You don't know, Mom … you don't know."

"Well, I know you don't get to decide, Randal. This is not your house."

"Well, it's my room. Fix up the guest room or something. She's not staying with me."

"Is there a problem?" Becca popped into the kitchen and asked.

"No, dear, Randal is just not feeling great. I've got a catering job tonight. I'll be out late. Her dad's out of town with work, and he won't be home until tomorrow, so you girls have plenty of time to talk and get reacquainted with each other. I know you've been in different worlds for a while," my mom said. Then she went over to Becca and whispered loudly, "You need to make her feel comfortable. Something's going on with her. She's all moody."

Becca winked. "Don't worry. I've got her, Mrs. Raines."

My mom headed to the garage and said, "Okay! Bye, girls."

I wanted to scream out, "Mom, are you serious? You don't even know the whole story with Becca, and you're leaving me here with her. She's a dyke! While that might not be the nicest of words, surely, Mom, you don't want anybody hustling me! And certainly not a girl." But I said nothing.

"Stay over there!" I threatened.

"Why are you tripping? Why are you fighting this?" Becca mused. "You don't wanna go there; I won't go there, but don't act like who I am is beneath you. As I told you before, you haven't even tried it. So don't knock it."

"Well, I'm not gonna try it. Now that I'm saying that, maybe you will leave on your own. I'm sick and tired of you being so sneaky, trying to push yourself into my life. You say you are not wanting to be forceful, but everywhere I turn, you're there. That's gross."

She reached into her pocket and pulled out a joint. "What your tail needs is a whiff of this."

"Excuse me?" I said, shocked.

"Don't try to act all goody-goody and girlie-girlie. Live a little, Randal. Your mom and I have been talking. She said you were depressed. I wanna get you out of your funk."

"By hitting on me? I told you I don't swing that way."

"Great, then when I get you relaxed, you have nothing to worry about."

"My mom doesn't allow that here."

"I'm not an idiot. I'm striking it outside. I'm not even trying to leave the smell in your place.

If you want to come out on the deck and join me, it will be our game."

Becca reached into her backpack and pulled out a lighter. It took her no time to open up the back door and step out onto the deck. She didn't even close the door. That's how sure she was that I was going to follow her. When I saw her through the window, taking a few hits, letting the smoke out into the breezy fall air, I realized that maybe the pot would help me forget my woes. Maybe taking a puff or two would allow me to relax and not be so stressed out. Maybe smoking weed for the first time was just what I needed to get the relief I craved.

Feeling crazy, I stepped out on the deck. Without saying one word or looking at me, Becca handed the joint my way. I coughed after taking my first puffs. She took it from me and showed me how to do it.

I started feeling my shoulders loosening up. I was laughing for no reason. It almost felt like I could fly. I guess I was high because I wasn't so uptight anymore. I wasn't completely oblivious to what was going on around me. I knew my name was Randal, and I was at my house. I was

alone with Becca. She started massaging my shoulders. The rubs she gave were even more blissful as I took more puffs. She put out the joint and put the leftovers in her pocket.

"No, no, no. I want to have a little bit more," I giggled.

"No, no, no. I think you had enough," she replied.

I knew my way to my room, but I was having a hard time figuring out the correct way to go. The world was spinning slightly. I think I needed to lie down.

"You know my house better than I do," I joked. "Take me."

When we got to my bedroom door, something told me not to go inside, but I couldn't recall why I shouldn't. Then Becca clutched my hand and gently pulled me toward her. She shut my bedroom door and pinned me against it.

"What are you doing?" I laughed.

I could feel her breathing on my neck as she kissed it. Then she kissed my cheek. Then her lips met mine. Without even thinking, I kissed her back. I couldn't jerk away. Once I realized

what I was doing, I did muster up the where-
withal to turn my head to the side. She thought
I wanted this. She placed her hand on my breast.
Did I want it? Her touch felt good. What was
wrong with me? I wasn't gay. If not, why was I
having this ludicrous feeling?

Completely Shattered

Everything Becca was doing to me felt great. I didn't know if it was me or if it was her or if it was the weed or if it was the feeling. Either way, I was swirling. As her tongue slid down my throat, my breathing increased. Her hands started roaming, and I started breathing even faster. What was happening to me? Why did I like this? Was the feeling so bad? Heck yes! I told myself to snap out of it. When my cell phone rang, I jumped away from Becca. I truly felt saved by the bell.

"Don't answer it," she ordered.

"No, I have to. You don't understand. I really need to get this," I said. I jerked away from her.

"No, don't go. Don't leave. You're enjoying yourself, right?" she questioned, clutching my hand.

I didn't even look at who was calling. I just quickly answered and put my hand out in front to stop Becca and said, "Hello?"

"Hey, Randal. This is ER. You got a second to talk?"

I had to shake my head at that moment. ER Stone was calling me. He wasn't gonna play me if that's what he thought. Did he want to have his cake and eat it too? I had talked to Jillian earlier, and I knew he was still her guy. Turning my back to Becca, I looked into the phone as if he could see how upset I was.

With attitude, I seethed, "Why are you calling me? Go call Jillian."

Though he was not able to see me, he certainly could hear that I was truly upset. Trying to defuse me, he said, "Wait, wait, wait, calm down. There is no Jillian."

"Please! Go tell that to someone else. I saw her today at the state cheerleading competition.

She told me all about the two of you guys being tighter than tight. Just leave me alone, ER."

"Randal, please wait! Don't hang up!"

"What do you want?" I quizzed.

"I really need to talk to you. I know it's late, but could I come swoop you up? We could hang out for a bit. You live near the school, right?"

"I didn't even agree that I would go out with you," I said hotly.

"Go out with somebody?!" Becca shouted. "You have company."

The thought of me spending more time with a shark like Becca wasn't comforting. Knowing she was pressuring me, I gave ER the address. He said he'd be at my house in ten minutes.

"Where do you think you're going?" Becca lectured like she was my mother.

"Becca, I didn't invite you over here. That was something that you and my mom cooked up."

"But you're enjoying yourself," she whined.

There was no need for me to argue with her. She was right. But just because something felt good didn't mean it was the right thing for you. My dad said that all the time, and now I knew exactly where he was coming from.

Both of my parents were away. Thankfully, I didn't have to worry about getting their permission to go out with ER. Besides, the way my mom was acting, she wanted me home with Becca and would have said no.

"How dare you go and just leave me here," Becca shouted. "Who is this guy? You and I can have something together."

"No, we can't have anything," I said, trying to shake off the thought of what I'd just done.

She tried to block my exit. I quickly stepped away. I looked around for something to smack her with, and I saw the broom. I wanted to whack her over the head to get her to understand there could be nothing between us. Ever.

"You shouldn't leave me here. Can't we even talk about this?" she begged. But there was nothing more to say.

As soon as ER showed up at my door, I flew out of the house. I didn't even take the time to say hello. Nor did I give him a hug or anything. I just wanted him to start the engine and jet. The last thing I needed was for Becca to come out and give ER all kinds of ideas. As we drove, I realized I wasn't the only one who was anxious.

"Sorry I called you on such short notice."

"No, it's fine. Everything okay?" I asked.

"I just didn't feel like being at home. I wanted to be around someone I thought could understand me."

"And I popped into your head?" I questioned.

"I'm not trying to be pushy, forward, or anything, but I've just been thinking about you."

How could that be? He had a girlfriend, and though he told me over the phone things were over, was I ready to believe him?

"I wanna get to know you better, Randal. And some of the stuff that Jillian and I went through was personal."

"I can appreciate that," I said. I didn't want him sharing anything if he wasn't comfortable.

He opened up a bit and said, "But I will tell you that she wasn't my type."

I looked away. I didn't want to be presumptuous and ask if *I* was his type. But he *called* me. He said that he wanted to hang out with me, and he said that I was the one person who he wanted to be with. So what did that all mean? Where was he trying to take this thing? Did I want him to take it anywhere?

"You know, maybe us hanging out and all isn't a good idea. You and Jillian could work things out."

"And though I didn't tell you the details," he said, "I do want to let you know it's over. No ifs, ands, or buts about any of that. I'm through."

"Maybe it's too soon for you to be getting into another relationship. But I'm not saying that's what you're saying," I explained, not wanting to look foolish.

He took my hand and squeezed it tight. "I'm not trying to go fast, but I'm feeling something."

At that very moment, I was feeling something too. He wasn't even kissing me, but just the touch of his hand sent me spiraling into fantasyland way more than Becca's kiss did. However, I couldn't shake the feeling that I had felt something from making out with a girl. Yeah, it could have certainly been the pot, but what if it wasn't? I couldn't get into a relationship with a guy when I could possibly feel something for a girl. At that moment, I wanted to take my fist and pound it on the dashboard.

"I can see I'm making you uncomfortable," he said, feeling my fidgety ways.

"I'm a just a little all over the place right now, ER. And why is your name ER anyway?"

"Because it's Edgar Remington Stone, and if you tell anybody, I'll have to hunt you down."

"Okay, but Edgar is not so bad," I countered. "Okay, maybe ER works better."

"I think you're beautiful, Randal." He touched my face. "And I just don't mean on the outside. You glow from the inside. You're sweet. You're always there for people. You're respectful to others. I guess I'm just a little tired of pushy people in my life, so much so that you stand out. Everywhere I go, it's like you're shining. I'm a magnet drawn to you, like I wanna be in your force field. You feel me?"

"I'm just *way* different from Jillian."

"Jillian is a phony and you … oh, uh, are you talking about your skin color? If I had a problem with color, I wouldn't be at Lockwood."

"Going to a black school and dating a black girl are two totally different things."

"I thought you were biracial. Your mom is white. My mom is white. What's the difference? And with the crazy relationships I've just been in with some white girls—"

"What? You've dated a lot of girls, huh?" I asked.

"Dating Jillian and her many moods was like dating twenty girls! But I know now that I need someone in my life with substance. I need someone who's not so broken that she can't help me keep it together."

"I think you've got the wrong girl," I said to him, knowing I'd been emotionally struggling lately. "I'm as shattered and confused as they come."

"Maybe we can help pull each other together," he offered.

He touched my cheek. I lost my breath and murmured, "Maybe we could."

My date was completely ruined when I looked down at my phone and saw that my mom was calling. I didn't really want to see this horror flick, but I was sitting in the dark theater with ER. My mom was supposed to be finishing up a party she was catering, not worrying about what was going on with me. I had a funny feeling that everything was not okay.

"Hello?" I whispered into the receiver.

"Shhh!" someone hushed.

I might not have been interested in the horror movie, but everyone else was. It was opening weekend and the place was packed. So when my mom started going off on me, I excused myself and stepped out into the hall. I didn't realize what a gentleman ER was; he followed me immediately. My mom had already heard a male's voice, and I wasn't in the business of lying to her. However, I didn't need ER to keep talking. Whatever she was imagining was drama enough.

I held the phone away from my face and whispered to ER, "I got this. I just need to talk to my mom real quick. I'll be right in."

"Randal Raines, can you hear me, girl?" my mom said with a little soul and spunk that I didn't know she had.

"Yes, ma'am, I'm right here."

"Well, you put me on hold for so long. Where are you? I'm thinking you're at home, entertaining Becca, but she calls me all hysterical."

My mom didn't need to say any more at that point. I knew right away what was going on. I wasn't responding to any of the little texts that Becca was sending me. So she reached out to my

mom, sending her into a panic to make sure I responded. Well, I needed to show my old friend who was boss.

So I said, "Mom, I told you it wasn't a good idea to have Becca come over. I had plans that I didn't even get to share with you because you were so adamant that I had to be there with someone who I didn't want to hang out with."

"You're not answering my question, Randal Raines. Where are you?"

"I'm at the movies with a friend."

"What friend?"

"This guy named ER. He goes to my school."

"A guy? I haven't even met this person. Does your dad know him?"

I so badly wanted to say, "Mom, he's white, unlike most of the boys here. He's not mixed like me, but white like you. Certainly, that should make him okay in your eyes and *way* better than me sleeping with a gay female who brought drugs into your house." But of course, I said none of that. I just gave her the answers she wanted to hear. She seemed satisfied and told me to be safe and come right home afterwards. Now *that* was what I wanted; no issues or worries coming

at me. I went right back into the theater and enjoyed myself.

"Everything okay?" ER asked.

I just showed my pearly whites. No worries. Not until I screamed at the frightening picture. Then ER held my hand.

"I got you. It's okay," he said.

And I really enjoyed clinging to his arm. Inwardly, I wanted to call my girls so bad. I had been looking for love, deeply wanting it. And when I wasn't searching, these crazy mixed-up emotions found me.

When we got out of the theater, ER asked me if I wanted something to eat. He wanted to spend more time with me. And I was thrilled, thinking we'd get a chance to know each other better. But I did realize I couldn't stay out too long because I needed to get home. Before I could respond, my arm was yanked away.

"What are you doing?!" ER yelled.

When I looked my assailant in the eye, I was furious. It was Becca. What was it now?

"What are you doing out here?" I hissed.

She smirked, "I came here to talk to you."

"What are you doing on this side of town?" ER asked.

"Do you want me to tell him or do you want to talk to me?" Becca threatened.

"I'll be right back," I said to ER.

"All right, I'll be over by my car," he replied skeptically.

Huffing, I started talking to Becca. "What are you doing? This is like stalking. This is crazy. You are nuts."

"You left me at your house."

"Well, obviously you're not stranded. You got your car."

"If my parents wanted me to drive all over town, they wouldn't have made sure I was at your house."

"I'm sure there're lots of things your parents don't know."

"You wanna call and ask them? You wanna rat me out? You wanna divulge my secrets? Trying to make me shake in my boots, are you? Well, two can play that game. You want me to tell that guy what we've been up to? No? Then I suggest you come with me," she grabbed my arm again.

"Just stop," I yelled.

"Why are you acting like you want me to stop? You weren't acting that way when we were in your room."

I had no reply to that remark. While I couldn't confirm that what she was sensing from me was real, I certainly couldn't deny it either. However, now I was clear I wanted to be with ER.

"I just need to talk to you, Randal. I know this all just seems extreme, and I know lots of stuff you're feeling is new. But if we could just go back to your house and chill, I know some of the aches you have will go away."

Emotions were running extra high at that point. I was running hot, ready to explode. Becca had me where she wanted me. I didn't know what her parents knew about her. I was sure ER didn't need to know about my recent actions.

I walked over to ER and said, "I'm sorry, but I've gotta go."

I didn't want him to ask what was wrong. I didn't need him to offer me a ride home. I just needed him to go before he actually found out how unstable I was. I barely knew him, but I could tell in his eyes that he was disappointed. I

so wanted to open up to him and tell him everything. I needed help. Was I straight? I could just imagine a kiss from him; a genuine kiss would let me know if I felt something for boys. But I didn't have the guts to truly confront any of what I was going through. So I left him there uneasy, and I walked away devastated. I was such a coward.

I couldn't believe that when I got home, I was pouting like a little baby. Becca wanted me to talk to her, but I didn't have to oblige her every wish. She kept talking and talking, but she didn't move me to speak. She made me return with her, but she couldn't make me talk. However, I was getting frustrated when the two things I thought might happen did not: One, I wanted her to just give up and go home. Two, I wanted her to shut the heck up and go to sleep. Either way, I wouldn't have to deal with her, but neither thing happened.

When she went to the bathroom, I realized I had to do something. I didn't have much time to figure it out, but I couldn't remain her prisoner. Becca was playing hardball, and I needed backup. I grabbed my phone and called Eva.

I didn't know if she would answer or not, but when she did, I said, "I know I'm the last person you want to hear from right now, and I'm so sorry things between us have gotten crazy. It wasn't me who blabbed about the video. I didn't tell anybody at that school."

"I know," she surprised me and said.

"What do you mean, you know?"

"Whitney admitted that people were talking about it on Facebook. Someone from our school sent a link to someone at Grovehill. It just spread from there. I shouldn't have been mad at you for something that I've done anyway."

"You didn't do anything. Rico did an awful thing to you. And now he's gonna pay."

"You are right, but still I can't act blameless in all of this, and I should have called you before. I've just still been so stressed."

Cutting to the chase, I said, "What are you doing now? I need your help."

"What's up? Name it and I'm there."

"I actually need you to come over to my house," I begged.

"Landon is on his way over here. He could swing me by there."

"Great, come help."

"What's up?" Eva quizzed.

I gave her the fastest version of all the craziness with just enough time to get off the phone before Becca came out of the bathroom. The two of us sat twiddling our thumbs. I guess she was trying to break me down, but that wasn't happening. Help was on the way.

We didn't turn on the TV. We didn't play any video games. We just sat still until the doorbell rang.

"That's not your mom. You don't need to get it," Becca ordered.

"This is my house. You can't tell me what I'm gonna do."

"Well, if it's that guy ... if it is that dude who used to go to my school ... I'm telling him if you open the door. So you better think twice."

"Quit threatening me," I ordered. I opened the door, and Eva stormed in with Landon behind her.

"Who are you?" Becca said to Eva.

Eva yelled, "Don't worry about who I am. I just came to set you straight. Girls like you, thinking they're all tough and manly, can bully

people into doing whatever they want. Well, your game is over with Randal."

"Oh, step out of my face, *sista*," Becca said, trying to be funny.

"Trust me, baby, I am not your sister," Eva snapped. "You don't want none of this. A real man is in the house."

Eva pointed at Landon. He just gave a boyish grin. I was out of the way.

"Yeah, like I'm really scared," Becca growled, looking over at Landon, unimpressed.

Eva stepped to her and retorted, "Oh, you don't need to be scared of him. You need to be scared of *me* because your tough little behind don't have nothing on my crazy, ghetto self. So try me now."

"This has nothing to do with you. So just take your little eye-rolling, gum-popping, loud-mouthing self back out the door you just came in from," Becca shouted. Then she pushed Eva just a little bit, which set off fireworks in my place.

"Landon, get her!" I screamed.

"Which one?!" he yelled out.

"Either one, and I'll grab the other," I said, feeling bad that I had started a fire.

"If Randal wants me to leave, she can open up her mouth and tell me she wants me to leave."

"I want you to leave," I screamed.

"You sure about that? You sure you want me to tell your friends *everything*?"

"Why are you threatening my girl?" Eva said, trying to get to Becca. "Get up off me, Landon. Get up off me! Im'a slap that bi—"

Landon said, "No, I'm holding you back, girl, before you lose it on this white heifer. She don't stand a chance with you in the house."

Becca said, "Please. She doesn't know me. I'm packing."

"Packing bluffs," Landon mimicked.

"What is all this commotion?" my mom thundered.

Usually, I could hear the garage door opening, but this time I was so focused on making sure my house did not come tumbling down that I was oblivious. My mom did not appear pleased.

"I just did what you asked, Mom," Becca said sweetly, like she was Miss Pure and Innocent. "I went and found Randal and brought her home safely so she wouldn't have to ride with that ER guy."

At that moment, my eyes got wide because Eva and Landon looked at each other like, *Um, she was out with ER? Say what?*

"Long story," I shrugged.

"Oh, what? They didn't know you were on a hot date with that white boy? Did I blow your cover? Is that taboo?" Becca asserted, clearly desperate and dumb.

"No, I think it's real cool," Landon said. "I'm just surprised I didn't know, but let's go so we can talk about all this. Your mom is home. Talk to her. We need to go."

"Randal doesn't need to go anywhere. Her mom just got in," Becca continued, acting protective. She truly deserved an Oscar. "Mom, what am I gonna do if Randal's gone?"

My mom could tell that something wasn't right with Becca. Becca looked manly, and my mom had never seen her that way before. I could tell that my mom was also put off by Becca's clingy ways, but she still didn't say anything. She didn't tell me I could go. She wasn't on my side.

I grabbed my purse and coat, kissed her on the cheek and said, "I'm out of here, Mom. Landon will bring me back later."

"You're not going anywhere," Becca ordered. My mom glared at her. "I mean, your mom hasn't told you that you could go anywhere." Becca's backpedaling was not working.

"Randal, what is going on? I've never seen you this forceful. What are you doing?"

There was so much I wanted to tell my mom about Becca so she could completely understand that she wasn't the person she thought she was. Becca was clearly not a pageant girl any longer. And if my prim and proper mom knew all the facts, she wouldn't want me to hang out with this girl with the split personality. However, I knew I needed to get out of the house. I really wanted to find ER and salvage any chance I had with him.

I looked at Becca and her eyes turned red. I knew if I didn't get out of there fast, she was going to tell everybody that we fooled around. I didn't know how much she would embellish. So when my mom tried to stop me, I slammed the door in her face.

"Come on, girl. You can apologize later," Eva said.

Everything was messed up. I had walked out on a guy I possibly had feelings for. I had

disrespected my mom, and the girl who liked me way too much was blackmailing me. Yep, add all of that to my identity crisis, and I'd say that my world was completely shattered.

CHAPTER 6

Decided Path

Dang, Randal, I didn't know you were hanging with my man ER," Landon said as soon as we got into his ride.

"Yeah, and I want every detail," Eva said. But Landon looked over at her sternly.

"Okay, okay, somebody's bringing out the best in you," I laughed.

"Ha-ha-ha. Now give me the scoop on when he called you," Eva ordered.

"It doesn't matter anyway. He probably won't speak to me ever again," I pouted.

"I don't know what happened, but ER is one of the truest brothers I know, which is too funny because he's not even a brother. Really though,

if I had to go into a battle, I wouldn't go into it without him," Landon said to me, giving me insight on the guy who had me spinning.

Eva leaned over to Landon and whispered something. I leaned back to reflect. While it was sort of gangster, leaving my house and practically ignoring my mom, I was proud I did it. And I would do it again. I'd been drowning these last couple of weeks. That bold action showed that I was ready to live. I didn't want anyone pushing me around. I wasn't going to let anyone control me. While everything in my life wasn't exactly figured out, knowing that life mattered was a huge start.

"I'm not hungry, guys," I said when we pulled into an IHOP restaurant.

"Trust me, you want some pancakes, sausage, eggs, bacon, something. C'mon, get out," Eva said, opening the car door.

Landon didn't wait on us. He gave us the peace out sign. He then turned and went inside the restaurant.

"What's going on?" I asked.

"Don't freak out, but ER is here," Eva told me with a sly grin.

"He doesn't wanna see me," I shouted. I quickly tried to shut the car door.

"Do you wanna see him?" she asked, holding out her hand to help me out.

"Desperately," I cried.

"Well then, let's go do it. Too many times we don't go for it all because we're afraid to fail. I've been wanting to call you all day to apologize for overreacting. I was tripping. I got timid, thinking you would be too mad at me, so I refrained from doing what I knew what was right in my heart. It was so funny because I kept thinking about you. Then you called me. Now that we're back, cool. I'm gonna do what you said the four of us haven't been doing, and that's care about Randal's business like we care about our own. So you go and talk to Mr. JR, GQ, ET or whatever his name is."

"It's ER," I chuckled.

"Okay! Well, you and Mr. ER Stone need to talk."

I hugged her until I heard ER's voice call me. "Randal? Landon said you're out here to see me. Everything okay?"

Eva stepped away from our embrace and waved ER's way. "Ah, ER, over here. It's Eva."

"Yeah, hey," ER said.

Eva shook her head and went from nice to naughty. "I don't know what's going on with you and my girl, but let's be clear, white boy. You're a boy, and you've got one of them things between your legs, and it needs to stay in your pants. Randal is a sweet girl. You get what I'm saying?"

"Eva," I gasped, swatting her.

"What?" Eva yelped.

I pushed her toward the restaurant door. She laughed and waved. I smiled and shooed her away.

ER wasn't grinning. I knew that wasn't a good sign. He was angry with me. There was no way I could explain this other than being transparent. But if he saw all of me, I was sure we'd be over.

On an impulse, I reached over to his neck, pulled him toward me, and kissed him. At first we were in rhythm, and I was happy to discover that I was feeling something. But then he abruptly pulled away. Both of his hands were on my arms. He didn't shake me but he was stern.

"Okay, you gotta talk to me. I'm not some toy, Randal. I thought we were having a good

time. You left with no explanation. Now you're kissing me. What the heck?"

I started shivering. He asked me if I wanted to get in his car. I nodded. I texted Eva to let her know we were still outside and headed to his warmer car. She texted back and told me to let her know if she needed to come out and watch my back. That meant so much.

"Are you gonna talk to me?" he asked when we got inside the car.

"I don't know where to begin," I opened up my heart and said.

"If you wanna let me in, just talk. Like why you were with Becca. She's—"

"What? Gay?" I finished "Yeah okay, let me just lay it all out there. She's spending the night at my house. She came over earlier. She came on to me. Here is the thing; we shared a joint. I was feeling more relaxed than I probably have been in my life, which is why I'm sure people do drugs, but it impaired me. I kissed her."

"Did you like it?" he asked without any judgment in his voice.

"I don't know. I know deep down in my soul I don't want a relationship with a girl. Same-sex

relationships may be for some people, but it is not for me. So that's why I kissed you. I wanted to feel something."

"Did you feel something?" he asked, touching my brow.

I took his hand and kissed it softly, "Yes." Quickly letting go of his hand, I said, "That information probably scares you, huh? As if Jillian wasn't crazy enough, I have all kinds of issues: Don't know if I'm gay or straight. Don't know if I'm black or white. Don't know if I'm coming or going—just flipping mixed up."

"Who has it all together?" he wondered.

"You do."

"I was dating Jillian. I couldn't be that self-assured," ER joked. We both shared a laugh. "I want to tell you something that I'd like you to keep in the strictest confidence."

I smiled. He nodded. We were in agreement that he could share anything, and I'd keep it to myself.

"I didn't even know why my dad moved me. It was so abrupt. He didn't want me to live with my mom anymore, and the two of them have been arguing over it. They have been divorced for a few

years. I went over to her place to find out what was going on. She didn't know I was coming, and I found her with another woman. Talk about your world turned upside down. The situation no way compares to your experimenting after smoking a joint. My mom's a lesbian. That's why my parents divorced. That's why I called you earlier tonight. I'm just having a hard time taking it."

I reached over and hugged him. We just held each other. We didn't have answers. We weren't trying to get rid of the problem, but in that embrace, I knew we were connecting. I knew ER Stone was the guy for me.

"How could you do this to me, Randal? How could you just run out? Your brother would never be so rude to me," my mom screeched.

I was super excited when ER dropped me off because I didn't see Becca's car. I didn't feel bad one bit. If her parents were truly out of town, she had plenty of other friends she could go hang out with. Wherever she was, as long as it wasn't at my place, I was fine.

Whatever my mom wanted to dish out to me, I could take because that crazy bully was gone. I

really didn't think Becca was that awful, but she needed to learn that *no* means *no*. She could be whatever sexual orientation that she wanted.

When Mom heard me enter, she started yelling and screaming. She needed to settle down. She needed to calm down. She needed to hear me out.

I said, "Mom, if you wanna talk, we can do that."

"Okay, let's talk," she suggested and indicated the couch. "I'm going to set up an appointment for you to go see a therapist next week. Randal, I'm not just going to tolerate disrespectful behavior. When your dad finds out that you just walked out on me, he's not going to be happy."

It was my mom's job to run things by my father. The two of them were raising me; I got that. But I was a little hypersensitive to people throwing pronouncements in my face. I thought she was going to listen to me tell her what was up, but she started venting again. I let it go in one ear and straight out the other. I sat there with a smirk on my face.

I focused on the fact that ER and I had started connecting. On the drive home, he held my

hand. He told me that what I was going through did not make him turn around and run in the opposite direction. He even revealed to me that he was extremely nervous about the upcoming playoff game. From what I heard, the guy had mad skills. However, he was humble, and I told him he had nothing to worry about because he was going to kick the game-winning field goal. I could just feel it. Of course we had no clue about what the future would hold, but I knew what it was like to be nervous, and I definitely wanted our football team to do better than our cheer squad did at the state competition.

"Are you even hearing me, Randal?" my mom called out, snapping me back into reality.

"Yes, Mom, but you're sort of saying the same thing over and over again."

"You had company over here. A young lady that used to be your best friend, and for the life of me, I don't understand why you ran out on her. I tried to get her to tell me, but she gave no response."

"Good, so you asked her," I said. I was excited that my mom asked Becca the tough questions, because for some reason Becca was playing the

role like everything was great, like she was a role-model friend and still the sweet girl my mom remembered.

Why didn't she want my mom to know that so much about her had changed? As I thought about it, I wondered why she only threatened to tell ER what was going on, but she never mentioned telling my mom. Maybe her parents were clueless about their daughter's sexual orientation. Interesting.

Well, I wasn't going to let it go that Becca was posing as the good one. Granted, I wasn't perfect, but I was closer to being good than Becca was. It was about time my mom knew.

"Are you ready to hear this?" I asked, grabbing her hand.

"Hear what?"

"Mom, you think Becca's the same girl she was years ago. You think she's my sweet friend that you used to buy Barbie dolls for."

"I know, wasn't that cute? I bought y'all matching Barbie dolls."

"Mom, Mom, Mom, Becca was pretending with you."

"I don't understand."

"Again, Mom, can we talk? 'Cause I don't want you to freak out on me. I'm trying things."

"What do you mean, trying things? What did you and that young man do? I saw him pull up into the driveway. Was that ER? You have to watch young men. They will tell you what you want to hear, and before you know it, they will be trying to have their way with you."

"Mom, let me just explain. You are worried about the wrong person."

"So you and this boy kept things strictly platonic?"

"I don't wanna lie to you, Mom. I kissed him."

"See, and where do you think that leads?"

"Mom, Becca *kissed* me. Which do you think is worse?"

My mom looked dumbfounded. I hated to burst her bubble. I'd exposed her best friend's daughter. It was time. All right, I'd already started, so I might as well finish.

Giving her all the details, I said, "Becca knows she's gay. She had the hots for me. She wanted to spend the night so she could seduce me. Connect the dots, Mom."

"What do you mean? Did you kiss her back? Do you think you're gay?"

"No, Mom, I'm not gay. Um, she did bring a joint over here," I mumbled.

"You had smokes in my house?" she vented.

"No, Mom, it was outside, but yeah, I tried it," I said.

She gave me a disappointed glare. "Either way is bad, Randal Raines."

"Okay, I won't do it again. I learned a lesson, trust me. I couldn't even really think straight, and when I was vulnerable, she took advantage of me. She manipulated you by calling and telling you all sorts of things. That's why I wanted to get away. I wasn't trying to disrespect you intentionally. I love you, Mom. I know I've given you and Dad a hard time about trying to find my way and trying to figure out if I'm black or if I'm white. Well, I've come to the realization that I'm just Randal, made up of a great mixture of a whole lot of stuff."

Tears fell from my mom's face. I did not know if she was upset about how she misjudged Becca. I hoped she was emotional because I was getting my head back on straight.

I took her hand and said, "I'm just a teen-ager who struggles like so many others in the world. I'm from a good family, and my parents love me. While I'm gonna make some stupid choices, I know I've got a mom who I can take my problems to. I've got a great dad who can steer me straight. And I got some good girlfriends, like Eva, Charli, and those guys. While I have been a little pigheaded and caused some dissension between us, they got my back in a crunch."

"Yeah, they love you."

"They do. Eva and I have worked it out. I haven't spoken to Charli, Ella, or Hallie, and I don't know if they will even talk to me."

"What's going on with them? Why are you all so upset?"

"They just overheard some girl from Grove-hill talking about black kids at Lockwood."

"You didn't say anything bad about the girls?" Mom frowned.

"No, I didn't. I was just trying to get the other girl to hush, but stuff got out of control. I turned around and they were standing right there. It's for sure a misunderstanding. I now wanna clean it up, but I just thought they were

selfish—all about them and never about me. But I realized right now that all of us are kids, and it should be all about ourselves as we try to figure out a way. I don't know, maybe I'm not as mixed up as I thought."

"You're not," she said, opening her arms wide and enveloping me in the biggest hug.

"I apologize for thinking I knew what was best for you without all the facts. Thank you for trusting me with the truth. I'm proud of you, Randal. My baby's growing up."

Those words made me feel better than any romantic kiss I'd received in the last twenty-four hours. Knowing my mom was proud of me made me feel responsible. It made me feel loved, and that feeling was one I knew I never wanted to fade.

The school week passed, and I was feeling better than I had in a long time, and rightfully so. Things weren't perfect, but they were surely looking up. My mom and I had a great connection. I had a guy who smiled my way all week. Tonight was the night of the Lions' first playoff game, and we were hosting it at our own stadium.

While I had been tripping about the loud noises our crowd made compared to other schools, I was feeling the vibe. When we were in line on the field holding up the sign that the players would break through, Eva came over to me. She nudged me in a playful way.

Eva teased, "Somebody's smiling from here to California."

I just smiled wider. "I'm actually tired of being down."

"Please, Mr. ER has got you grinning."

"Can y'all hold up the signs right and line up to cheer, not gab?" Charli yelled.

I knew she wasn't frustrated with Eva. She was still salty with me. I had tried to get with the three of them throughout the week to apologize, but they weren't even hearing me out. So I made a decision to push on without their friendship. Shoot, Eva was all I needed anyway. Truth be told, she thought the three of them, including her sister, were a little stuck up.

"We're not missing a beat, Charli. Turn around and mind your business," Eva sassed.

Charli rolled her eyes and huffed. Hallie and Ella gave me looks that could kill. Gosh, they

were bringing me down—so down it was like I was standing at the bottom of the Grand Canyon.

Eva said, "Don't worry about them, they will come around. Hopefully they will, and if they don't, I got you."

"Yes, you do," I agreed, as the two of us started dancing and chanting and cheering.

I looked over and saw ER warming up for the big game. I noticed his practice kicks weren't going through the uprights. He was fussing with the holder. I clapped my hands together and hoped he would work out his inner turmoil.

He and I hadn't talked a lot all week. He said we would go out after the game. My mom had already given me permission to go out with him. I was super excited. Last thing I wanted was for him not to do well; then the night that I dreamed of would be bad. I wanted to go over there and say, "It's gonna be okay. You're gonna do really well. No worries. No stress. No strife." But Coach Woods always made sure we didn't fraternize with the football players after they ran through our sign. They barely tore it, which was a bad omen. Everyone knew you were supposed to smash the sign to pieces.

"That's a sign! We're gonna lose," Hallie groaned. "C'mon, Amir, y'all gotta do good."

"Don't say we're gonna lose," Charli fumed.

The two of them were a handful. I wanted to go and give them both big kisses on their cheeks and tell them to relax. We were gonna do great. This was going to be wonderful. To the Georgia Dome, here we come, but now it was kickoff time. I stood on Eva's shoulders with my pom-poms like I normally did, swirling them around in the air when the ball was kicked to us. Amir was supposed to catch it and run it back. He touched it, but it went through his hands, and the other team's linebacker scooped up the ball and ran it for a touchdown. Just like that, the visiting team scored. Their crowd went wild; our crowd booed.

I cheered, "That's okay! That's all right, boys! Let's win this game tonight!"

Everyone looked over at me like I was crazy, but I had to pep up the team. When they kicked the ball off to us the second time, and Amir was back there again, I saw Hallie holding her breath, hoping her boyfriend would redeem himself. He caught the ball, but he got tackled and let the ball go. There was a fumble. They didn't get to

run the ball again, but they did have the ball at our fifteen-yard line. On their second play, their quarterback threw the ball to a wide receiver. Amir was defending him. But the wide receiver caught the ball in the end zone.

Hallie whined, "My baby is having a horrible game, y'all. Oh my gosh, I should have never said anything about losing the game. I certainly didn't mean to bring anything bad on my boo."

I wanted to go over, shake her, and say, "They are playing. There is nothing superstitious going on with the Lions. Chill out! Don't worry! No strife!" But as the game went on, our team kept sucking.

With less than twenty seconds left on the clock in the fourth quarter, the score was the Patriots 14 and our Lions 13. We were on their thirty-five-yard line. We had the chance to kick the ball through the uprights and win the game. ER went out there, but his kick went wide left. The remaining seconds ticked off of the clock, and their team poured onto the field. We lost.

I wanted to go over and grab ER and hold him when he took off his helmet, slammed it to the ground, and dropped to his knees. I could see

that his face was red. My heart broke for him and the other guys. Other cheerleaders started crying too. This was our last game. We'd gone undefeated all season, but now it was over.

To see Whitney sad really made me aware that this was the end of her high school football days. This was the end of her Friday night lights. This was the end of a special time in a young person's life. Next year, that would be me.

I needed to seize every bit of it. I would miss the wins, the losses, the cold fall breeze blowing on my face, cheering with my pissed-off friends, the smell of the popcorn, and the band playing our school song. My eyes shifted back to ER. I was starting to feel something for him, and it melted my heart when I saw him breaking. Everyone needed to come back so he could kick again.

Later on, we were sitting in his car. He wasn't talking. He was so frustrated, but I just leaned over him and started letting my lips do some magic. I unbuttoned my blouse. When his hands didn't touch me, I wanted to get him out of his funk. So I started kissing his neck and put his hands on my bra. Then I started unbuttoning his pants and sliding my hands in places they

had never gone with anybody, but he quickly pulled back.

"Randal, what are you doing?" he sighed.

"I wanna make you feel good," I said, being honest with him.

"Is this about the gay thing? You wanna prove to yourself that your not."

I didn't answer. I wasn't consciously thinking that, but maybe that was something that was going on within me. I started shaking my head, trying to dismiss his accusation.

"We haven't talked about this, Randal, but you're a virgin, right?"

At that moment, I went back over to the passenger side and started fixing my clothes. "Yeah. And so? That doesn't mean that I can't *do it*."

"Well, that means that you shouldn't right now. I am too, okay? And I like it that way. I'm all bummed out because of the game. I appreciate you trying to cheer me up. When it's our time, it's gonna be something special, not something rushed and awkward. You deserve better than that. I deserve better than that. Can we make a pact to wait?"

"Sure," I sniffed, as he gently wiped the tears from my eyes.

"Don't get me wrong. I care for you a lot. You deserve the best. I want you to be my girl. I want us to wait. Is that okay with you?"

I nodded and smiled. I accepted his offer to be his girlfriend, and it was very appropriate. We'd both been in a rocky place, but I was giddy that we agreed on a decided path.

CHAPTER 7

Pleasures Abound

You ready to do this?" I asked ER. We had just pulled into Lockwood's parking lot Monday morning.

He smiled my way and told me to stay put. Like a first-class gentleman, he opened my door and escorted me through the parking lot. He held my hand while we walked toward the front entrance. I sighed. I could not believe Randal Raines had a beau!

I could feel eyes on us. I could hear gossip spreading about us. I was getting nervous. He squeezed my hand tighter.

"Are you sure you're ready for this?" he questioned. I nodded, and he opened the front door to the school, still not letting go of my hand.

I had to admit, I liked being with him. I liked that he was aware of what I was feeling. Truly, he was not pretending to be chivalrous; that's just who he was. Edgar Remington Stone was my guy, and I just needed to get backbone and enjoy the stroll, which I did once I stopped being so sensitive to everything going on around me. We almost made it to my locker without incident. Then, I heard an obnoxious voice.

"Well, well, well, ain't this a trip," Waxton quipped.

"You're standing in our way, Waxton. Move," ER demanded. Hmm, was this a little déjà vu?

Wax charged, "You don't own the halls, and you certainly don't own me. I can stand where I want to stand."

"I don't have no problem if I need to move you," ER retorted. The crowd grew around us.

"You couldn't even kick the extra point. Puleeze … 'Cause of your tail, we lost the game."

I felt ER trying to let go of my hand, but I squeezed it tighter and grabbed his arm.

"Don't even let him get to you."

"Yeah, listen to your girl," Wax taunted. He then looked over at me with hatred. "You are stupid enough to think a white boy is better than me. What's wrong with your tail? I always knew your boojie behind thought you were better than us anyway. Gotta little bit of white in you, and you think you better than all us around here."

"Step off!" ER ordered, putting his hand square in the middle of Waxton's chest.

Seeing I was ticked, Wax tried a softer approach. "I was dreaming about you, Randal. Why it gotta be like this? Why you choose him over me? White ain't right. When he gets tired of playing with the caramel, he's gonna toss you out like the trash."

"How about I throw you out?" ER ranted, grabbing Wax's shirt and pinning him up against the nearest locker.

"Fight, fight!" someone yelled.

"White boy, don't play!" someone screamed.

"We know he can't play football," a third guy yelled.

I could tell all the name calling was really getting to ER. It was one thing to be different,

but to have it thrown in your face every time you turned around was truly annoying. Why couldn't we all just be without labels and such?

ER said something to Waxton. I could not make out what it was. Immediately, Wax calmed down.

"All right, man, all right," Waxton said, trying to get ER's hands off of him.

"I'm just saying, do I have to go there or are you going to settle down? You need to get some help," ER said to him.

I asked, "What's going on with him?"

"I know he's doing drugs," ER whispered to me reluctantly.

I didn't want to be judgmental. Not too long ago, I smoked a joint myself, but the concern in ER's eyes let me know that it was more than just a dabble Wax was into. Out of the nowhere, Waxton returned and hit ER from behind. Both of us turned quickly. He certainly was on something because he was acting spacey and weird.

Landon ran up to Wax and said, "Man, I know it's gotta be tough dealing with the fact that you let a lot of folks know Gunn molested you too, but chill out, man."

I covered my mouth at that point because Waxton was the toughest boy in our school. I had been so out of touch with the latest that I hadn't heard that Wax was also one of Gunn's victims.

"You don't know nothing, man. You can't figure Wax out," Wax vented, referring to himself in the third person.

Landon said, "I know you don't need to be in this school high. I get you're stressed out because the memories won't go away. Been there, done that, man. I know what you're feeling, but you can beat this, and you don't need drugs to do it."

"You don't know what's going on with me. You don't know a thing about me. You don't know what I need. Get off me!" Wax said. He gave Landon a hard shove.

Landon followed him. ER wanted to do the same, but Landon said, "I got this, man. Stay with your girl."

"What's going on here?" Dr. Sapp yelled. "I don't even want to know. Be a shame to suspend people before the Thanksgiving break. So get to class right now!"

Landon and ER looked at each other like they wanted to tell our top administrator something.

Or they suspected that he already knew something. I couldn't figure it out. It was guy stuff. Wax was a butt, but they were trying to take care of his tail. And I admired that.

"I gotta get to class," ER said, leaning over and kissing me. "You all right?"

Giving him a slight grin, I nodded. Then I touched his arm and thanked him. I didn't want to leave his side. What a fun new feeling it was to care for a guy.

Eva had math with me, and as soon as I got in the class, she tugged on my arm.

"Word is out that you've been walking and holding hands with ER. Dang, girl, you decided to let the whole school know y'all are an item? That's what's up."

I couldn't respond before class started, and my head was spinning. Waxton, the big man on campus, was on a drug track to nowhere.

"Oh my gosh! How dare he come to my cheer banquet with *her*?" Charli squealed. Her dad walked into our gym, which was turned into a banquet facility, with a lady who was not her mom on his arm.

When she spotted her father, I was the closest to her. When she rushed out to the bathroom, I immediately followed her, all the while trying to talk myself out of speaking to her. She hated me and I knew it, but I also knew I loved her, and I wanted to fix things. I wanted to explain why I was tripping. I wanted to be there for her.

When I opened up the bathroom door, she screamed, "Randal, get out! Like I need you in here pretending. Get out of here, Randal!"

I wasn't going anywhere. I walked closer to her and let her yell at me until her head rested on my shoulder. For a minute I thought I had gotten her to trust me, to realize I cared, but she pushed me hard when the door opened. Hallie, Eva, and Ella rushed in to see what the problem was.

"Get her away from me," Charli hissed, like I had a disease or something.

I rushed over to Eva and insisted, "I just wanted to help. I just wanted to talk to her."

"You need to get out like she said," Hallie ordered. "Coming in here like you're all concerned. Your words spoke louder than your actions. We heard you say what you really think

of us behind our backs, when you didn't know we were listening. Remember?"

I got teary at that moment. I needed them to listen to me. I wanted them to hear me out. All this needed to be fixed, but knowing this was impossible, I opened up the bathroom door to exit. I was surprised when Eva reached over my head, slammed it shut, and placed her back against it so I could not leave.

"Okay, let me just be clear. I don't know what's going on with you guys as to why y'all can't work this out, talk to each other, hear each other's sides, and move on, but nobody's getting out of this bathroom until we do."

"My dad is here with another woman, Eva, okay? This isn't about me working it out with Randal right now. My family's falling apart!" Charli yelled.

"Well, Randal is your family, and that's been falling apart for far too long. Fix this so we can fix that," Eva demanded, stomping her feet in frustration. She turned me around and said, "Go talk to them. Talk to them now."

I was really surprised and heartbroken when Ella, the sweetest girl I knew, said, "I

143

don't wanna hear anything she has to say. We all know you're dating a guy now. It's all around school. You're with ER. But my thing is, is that really real or are you just using him because you are jealous of what we have."

"You know it's real," Hallie remarked. "The boy is w-h-i-t-e. Clearly, the girl ain't trying to get with a brother. That goes to solidify that she can't stand us."

"Okay, enough," I cried, wiping my own tears and finding my own voice. "Sure, you heard me say I had identity issues. Yes, I was bummed that my white mother doesn't think I am white. But I don't hate being black. It's just that black isn't totally who I am. I've only been in this neighborhood for two and a half years. I grew up around white kids and then suddenly things changed. I'm exposed to a different culture, different people, and it was a lot. But I don't hate it."

"Please," Charli said. "Talk to the freaking hand, like we believe you."

"I don't hate it, Charli." I went over and grabbed both of her hands and held them tightly so she couldn't jerk them from my grasp. "Being away from you guys for the last couple weeks

has allowed me to see that while I thought I didn't know *me*, I've actually got a great handle on who I am. I've struggled for so long. You have no idea because I was always so quiet. I missed you guys so much. I can't stand that girl y'all saw me talking to at the regional cheerleading competition. She was going on and on about how black girls act, and I just wanted her to shut up, so I just mumbled something to move her along."

"That's real smart. Push us under the water so you could step on our backs and cross the broken bridge."

"I realized I was wrong. The moment I saw you guys standing there, I realized I was wrong. I should have said something then, but I was a coward. I am not that girl anymore."

"But, Randal, you're even a little embarrassed by some of our actions," Ella said. "I see you sometimes when we're chanting, working it, and enjoying ourselves; you look at us like it's the worst thing."

" 'Cause in my opinion there's a time and a place for everything, and sometimes you guys just turn it on regardless of what the protocol should be."

"But who determines the protocol?" Hallie yelled. "You? Other white folks?"

Eva said, "Come on, y'all gotta admit sometimes we can get real raunchy. Last I remember, Randal's been there for all you guys. She's given you grace. She's been by your side."

"Ha," Charli said, walking far away from me.

Eva continued, "Okay, you guys might not know this because you weren't around. For example, Charli, when you lost your mind and were mad at all of us when you first got elected cheer captain, it was Randal who got in our faces and told us not to turn on you. Hallie, when you were out looking for your mom, it was Randal who wanted to organize a search party. And Ella, when you came home from the hospital and were resting from your gunshot wound, it was Randal who held your hand while you slept."

I couldn't believe Eva was being so real with them. I had done those things because it was just in me. I didn't usually say a lot, but I certainly had a big heart. I loved them. Eva looked at me like, *Okay, you're up.*

I walked over to the three of them and said, "I'm sorry I hurt you guys. I'm sorry that I didn't

respond like you thought I should. I'm sorry I didn't respond how I knew was right, but I care for you guys. I do need you to accept me, flaws and all."

"Come here," Charli encouraged, reaching to hug me tight. It felt so good to be close to her again. We cried in each other's arms. Hallie joined the embrace. Ella stroked my back.

"I missed you," Hallie said. "Forgive me, too, for being so judgmental. You've always been there for me the last few years. I was able to vent to you and talk about my mom. She's getting out of rehab soon. I don't know if she'll make it, but I know I need all of you guys in my life to help me either way."

"Yeah," Charli said. "And my dad's bringing that ... I don't know the words to describe *her*."

"Yeah, all that you're thinking," Eva acknowledged. "And more."

"Right," Charli said. "How could he bring *her* here? I certainly need my girls to deal with this. Obviously my parents' marriage is over. Going into the holidays and the New Year with them separated, I'm not going to be able to make it without y'all. Forgive me, Randal."

She kissed me on the cheek. Huge tears fell from my eyes. Were we really reconciling?

Ella came over to me and said, "I thought I remembered waking up one time and talking to you after my release from the hospital. I thought it was a dream. I remember you were in there with me when I was recuperating. I haven't told you guys, but I still can't sleep some nights thinking about getting shot. I wake up in a cold sweat. And I'm scared."

I reached over and hugged her. "It's okay. You're here. You're fine."

"I'm trying," Ella said, shaking in my arms.

Eva came over and said, "And, Randal, that first night I came in from the rape ... Everybody else was looking at me harshly, but I remember you came to the bathroom and wanted to talk. I so wanted to let you in, but I was ashamed. You were there and you cared. You knew something was wrong. I don't want the five of us to lose this bond. I'm blessed to have a twin sister, but there's something extra that the five of us share. We can't get in our own way and mess it up."

"Exactly," Charli said. "We're going to be seniors next year. And seniors rule the school."

We all smiled. We were all dealing with so much, but at that moment, we made a pact to be there for one another, to not get in our own way, and to help each other through whatever was to come. And that was better than any award or prize I could have received at the banquet.

It was Thanksgiving Day, and I was dreading it. I didn't want to hear my parent's fussing over whose family we were going to spend the day with. I didn't want to spend time with either set of grandparents. My mom's mom would talk about how fat I was getting. My dad's mom would tell me that I was too skinny.

I hated it that ER hadn't called me today. I knew he was still beating himself up for not making the field goal in the playoff game. While I couldn't understand how much it meant to him, I definitely didn't want him to be down. But this was a new Randal Raines. I wasn't going to let anyone rain on my parade. I just needed to suck it up and enjoy whatever the day would bring. I couldn't force ER to call me. I needed to be ready to talk to him whenever he came around. A confident me knew he would.

I smelled turkey and ham and something else that smelled awful. I got up, threw on my robe, and went into the kitchen. I was determined that even the yucky smell wasn't going to ruin my cheery attitude.

"Hey, Mom," I said, giving her a big hug.

"Hey, Randal."

"Uh, I know you know what you're doing in here, but why are you cooking so much food? Do we have to take stuff to Grandma's this year?"

I didn't identify which grandmother. Both of them always had a spread and never wanted my mom to bring a thing. They would be insulted if she did.

"There is something that stinks really bad, Mom. Please don't be mad at me, but what *are* you cooking?"

My dad came around the corner with the biggest grin on his face. "Hey, pumpkin," he called out.

"Hey, Dad."

"Smells good in here, huh?"

I didn't know what was wrong with his nostrils, but there was definitely a problem. He

went over to the pot and lifted the lid. He took a big whiff of the horrible smelling concoction.

"She's cooking chitlins!" He was all excited, like he had just won the lottery.

I was so surprised. "No way! Really?"

"Yep, and yams and greens. I sampled them this morning. We're gonna have the best Thanksgiving ever right here," my dad boasted.

"We're not going out this year?" I asked my parents.

"Nah, didn't you hear him, sis? We're staying right here and having our own family Thanksgiving," my brother Danton said, surprising me.

"When did you get here?" I swung around and gave my big brother a huge hug.

"I didn't think I was going to be able to come because we've been doing some stringent conditioning for baseball."

My brother was on scholarship at the University of Georgia. I missed him terribly. As a junior there, he had been gone from our daily routine for a couple years. Just having him back, seeing him there, and knowing he was around made me truly thankful.

"So go ahead, get dressed," my dad ordered.

"It's time to eat already?" I asked with shock.

"Yes, it's twelve thirty, sleepyhead" my mom added.

I said, "Oh my gosh, Mom, you let me sleep in! I would have helped."

"Well, Ms. Blount and Mrs. Black gave me some good recipes and taught me short cuts. I really didn't need any extra help, sweetie. Besides, you've been working hard all semester. And you've had a rough few weeks. I know you need to study some this weekend for your upcoming exams, and I just didn't want you to stress out. I want you to enjoy this special Thanksgiving. Pretty soon, you're gonna be like this one over here," she said, pointing at my brother, "away at someone's college. We won't have these days back." Then my mom started to choke up a little. My dad started rubbing her back.

I was stunned. I could not get my feet to move. For the first time in my seventeen years, my family was celebrating a holiday in the way I'd always envisioned.

"We are a family, Randal. There's lots of love in this house," my dad said, giving my mom a

flirtatious look. "We might not be able give you everything you need, but we certainly try. Now hurry up and get ready, 'cause I'm hungry."

So I dashed off, but just as I shut my door, my brother knocked on it. "Let me in. I need a word."

"Hey there, you," I said to him. I fake punched him in the gut a few times, like I was a boxer.

"You can't beat me. I don't know why you've always tried," he joked, making a motion like he was going to take a swing at me. I frowned. "Seriously, I know you got to get dressed. I just wanted to ask you what was going on with all this am I black or white stuff. You all right? You got Mom and Dad all in a tizzy."

While my brother should have understood because we had the same genetic makeup, he was a boy. He could be who he wanted to be and who would have cared? I could tell by the way he asked me that he didn't have issues about ethnicity. I loved talking to Danton. He was the type of big brother who could talk about anything; no question was ever too silly. He always made time for me, even when he was super busy with baseball. It's just now that he was in college, and

I was older myself, I didn't need him as much. Hmm, maybe I did need him.

I went and sat on my bed and said, "I don't know. I wish I could understand it. I mean, I'm feeling better about myself. My self-esteem is higher, but yeah, I struggled a lot lately. I was wondering where in the world I fit in."

"You fit in wherever you want to," he said. "Don't ever let anyone minimize who you are. People are mixed everywhere. Some places are more Hispanic, or Asian, or white, or African American. But even in those areas, folks are mixed with a little bit of this and a little bit of that. It might be that some are an eighth this, a fourth that, or a half whatever, but that's the way the world is going."

"So it doesn't bother you?"

"What?"

"Your racial makeup."

"Never. I'm proud of who I am. I know I got something unique to offer the world. If anybody's got issues with it, it's on them. Nobody can break you unless you let them. Randal, you've got a lot to live for. Don't let anyone push you around. You got me?"

I nodded and leaned over for a brotherly squeeze. I wished I was as mellow as Danton.

About an hour later, the four of us were seated, breaking bread. I still could not believe we were giving thanks at our own dining room table. The doorbell rang, and when my dad got up and answered it, a bunch of our family, black and white, flooded our home.

"What is going on?" my dad asked.

His mom said, "Well, when you didn't come over my house, I called *her* and asked when y'all were leaving so y'all could come over my house. And she said *she* was about to call me because she thought y'all were over my house. She wanted to know when y'all were coming over to her house. And so that's when we figured y'all were over here not wanting to split your time with either side. So we decided we're all gonna have Thanksgiving together here, whether you like it or not, Kenny. Danton's home, and we wanna see our baby boy and baby girl."

I was really a little down because I was enjoying just being with my immediate family. Then my mom's mom came over to me and said, "There she is, my Randal."

My dad's mom grabbed me and said, "Yep, she's *me*."

My mom's mom said, "Nope, she's *me*. No, she's the best of both of us."

In the middle of both of them, they hugged me. The two of them hadn't gotten along for most of my upbringing, yet here they were, letting me know I mattered. I felt so loved. Both sides of my family were laughing and eating together. I didn't think it could get much better.

But later that evening, the doorbell rang again, and I smiled when I saw ER. "Happy Thanksgiving. Your Mom said I could come over."

"You talked to my mom?" I asked.

"Yeah, you were with your grandmothers, so she just told me I could swing by. I'm not by myself, though." He moved out of the way, and I saw my girls.

I squealed, "Hey!"

They weren't alone. They had Blake, Amir, Landon, and Leo with them. Everyone filed in and started meeting my family. ER stood right by my side.

"Sorry I didn't call you earlier," ER whispered in my ear.

I kissed his cheek. "I'm just thankful to see you."

The guys went down to the basement with my brother after grabbing heaping plates of my mom's food. I pulled my girlfriends into my bedroom. I looked at them all and tears just started falling.

"This is the best day I've had in so long. Y'all just don't know. My parents had Thanksgiving here for me. My brother is home. My grandparents ended their bickering and decided to spend this holiday together. Then y'all came over with your guys. And there's a guy here who cares about me. I'm just overwhelmed."

"Well, quit crying 'cause we need to find out the scoop. Blake is here and not Brenton," Eva said, keeping it real.

"Oh, don't trip! You know the football players wanna spend time together," Charli said, trying to downplay the situation.

"Like Brenton doesn't ball," Eva snorted.

We went downstairs and had fun playing Taboo. Girls against guys, and you know who won. As my friends were gearing up to go, I reflected on the day. My brother was right. I had to be happy

with me, regardless of what anybody else felt. My grandmothers touched my heart when they told me I was the best of their heritage.

I figured I was like a delicious yellow cake with chocolate frosting—a whole bunch of things mixed together: sugar, fudge, flour, eggs, milk, butter, but when prepared the right way, like my mom does with every meal she serves, the mixture is splendid.

I was ready to seize what life had to offer. I was attending a great school. My family was solid and supported me with firm but loving authority. I cared for my friends from the bottom of my soul. And I had a guy who made my heart flutter. But all of these things meant nothing until I learned to love myself, and just like biting into that delicious dessert, loving myself is where unexpected pleasures abound.